CLOCK STRIKES PARADISE

Clock Strikes
PARADISE

CLOCK STRIKES PARADISE

Island Escapes Series

ERIN BROCKUS

Edited by Lawrence Editing Services and J. Speck

Cover design by GetCovers

Ebook ISBN: 978-1-957003-45-0

Paperback ISBN: 978-1-957003-46-7

Chapter One

Clay

LIFE WASN'T A FAIRY TALE, but watching hard work pay off had to be one of its greatest rewards. I sat behind my desk and stared at the dark winter Manhattan skyline, lost in thought like usual. My office was empty and silent, the way I preferred it. But not for long—Elise would be here any minute. My assistant of three years, Elise, knew my habits and schedules by heart. She anticipated my every need before I voiced it, managing my life with ruthless efficiency.

My corner office was located on the top floor of a Manhattan skyscraper, offering me a stunning view of the city through the floor-to-ceiling windows. The decor was modern, bordering on harsh, with black leather couches, steel coffee tables, and abstract paintings adorning the walls. With two fingers, I smoothed my gray silk tie and ensured my navy-blue Armani suit was immaculate. It was.

Today was Christmas, though not a hint of the holiday was to be found, nothing to distract me from the task at hand. I had been in the office all day, my only break a Face-Time with my parents and brother to celebrate the holiday. They were together in Connecticut, but I couldn't spare the time to visit in person.

And my single-mindedness was about to pay off. Immensely.

A quick glance at my watch informed me it was nearly 5:00 p.m. I wasn't a monster. I'd arranged the meeting for late in the day to allow the two employees involved most of the holiday off.

After two raps at the door followed by my disinterested "Enter," one of the eight-foot double doors opened silently. Elise walked in, her light gray skirt suit and heels clicking on the marble floor. She set an agenda on the blotter before me and a freshly brewed espresso near my right hand.

"Good evening, Mr. Harmon."

Her voice was crisp and professional. I glanced up, taking in her appearance. Late twenties, chestnut hair pulled into a sleek bun, minimal makeup, dark-blue eyes hiding behind glasses. All business and worth every penny I paid her. She stared at her tablet, her focus solely on her work. There was no need for tiresome, pointless conversation about how we each spent our Christmases. Elise was efficient enough to be invisible, which I appreciated.

Looking back at my triple monitor display, I asked, "Are the Q3 reports ready for review?"

"Yes, sir, along with all the finalized proposals received."

I nodded and took a sip of espresso, the bitterness reviving my senses. "Send them to me."

She tapped on her tablet and within seconds, the reports appeared on my screen. I scrolled through the data, the result of what my brother Nate and I had built from nothing. Our software, Podium, had become the leading sports-betting app in the world. I was the brains of the operation and Nate was the face. Years of sacrifice and sleepless nights had paid off, except for the recent complication of my brother needing an emergency image rescue. Which he had been wildly successful with. Now it was time for both of us to reap the benefits.

I switched files, scrutinizing two competing offers for the company. I knew the proposals by heart, having spent several days poring over every detail. Just as my eyes began to lose focus, another knock sounded at my door. I didn't look up from my screen as Elise marched across the room and opened the door. She ushered in Bart Mayhew, our CFO. Bart's charcoal-gray suit showed some wrinkles and draped loosely on his ample frame. His wiry brown hair was slicked back in an attempt to appear polished, but it only made him look like an extra in a *Sopranos* episode.

"Merry Christmas," Bart said to me with a casual grin, sauntering into the room.

I bit back a sigh. "Likewise."

"Thanks for having this meeting." He rubbed his hands together. "It got me out of Christmas dinner with my awful sister and brother-in-law. I'd rather work. I can always count on you, Clay."

I'd had a momentary pang of conscience about calling the two of them in on Christmas Day, but time was running short, and I needed to ensure all was ready. "Let's get started."

I motioned them both to the black leather couches in my seating area and refused to show my irritation at his familiarity. Since Bart was a member of the executive team, I couldn't take too much umbrage at him using my first name. And I didn't need to like the man to work with him. Elise's lips pressed into a thin line as she took a seat on the couch opposite Bart. Collecting my tablet, I moved to a plush leather armchair and transferred the financials to a wall of monitors before us.

"All right," I began, commanding their full attention. "Everything is in order for the upcoming sale. We've completed our due diligence, and now it's time to finalize the transaction."

Ambition sparked in Bart's eyes, but he was more focused on his own personal gain rather than Podium's success. Fortunately for him, they were one and the same. Elise, on the other hand, remained poised and attentive, ready to assist.

"Both top offers have been sent over," I said, pulling up the information on the monitors. Bart and I spent the next hour analyzing the proposals, discussing pros and cons and debating our options. Elise quietly took notes as I sifted through the data.

I'd invited Nate to the meeting, but he'd only rolled his eyes and reminded me what day it was. I ignored the tightening in my stomach that I'd blown my family off. All three of them liked to point out that I worked too hard. But was it work when you enjoyed it? I had managed a video conference with Nate a week ago to narrow down the proposals to the final contenders.

"Keep a close eye on these two during the trip," I instructed Bart. "We need to ensure we choose the right path forward for Podium."

"Understood," he replied, nodding. "Both have accepted our invitation and will arrive tomorrow just after we do. Laurent Dubois is flying from Paris and Celeste Rhodes from Santa Clara. And my bags are all packed. I can't wait for some tropical sun."

I nodded. "Very well. Elise, ensure all necessary documents are packed."

"Of course, Mr. Harmon," she responded with a quick glance at me through her tortoiseshell glasses.

"The sale of Podium is going to be the biggest deal of my career." I sold my first tech company for two billion dollars at the age of twenty-six. Now, six years later, I expected Podium's sale to dwarf that. "Podium represents part of my legacy, and I plan on getting top dollar for it."

I stared at Elise and Bart in turn, gauging their reactions. Elise nodded briskly as she tapped on her tablet. Bart grinned and gave me a thumbs-up. I bit back the urge to snap at him. The man was a necessary evil.

"Dubois and Rhodes are offering strong numbers, but I need them hungry and excited." I leaned forward, tenting my fingers. "That's why I'm bringing them both down to Calypso Key Resort. At the same time. A little tropical hospitality might stoke some competition between them, and I'll accept their final offers there."

A glimmer of excitement flickered through me at returning to the Florida Keys resort. It had been Nate's and my favorite childhood vacation spot, though I hadn't been back in years. I leaned back against the plush back of my armchair. "Elise, you're vital for keeping everything on schedule and running smoothly behind the scenes. Ensure you're ready to go first thing in the morning."

As much as I saw Elise as merely a cog in my business machine, I couldn't deny her competence. I suspected the resort trip would tax even her unflappable capability. Her eyes widened at my announcement and her fingers froze above the tablet. Then she nodded briskly before sending Bart a long side-eye. "Of course, sir."

I raised my gaze to stare at the city lights again. As cutthroat as I was, part of me was sad to sell the business my brother and I had built. But Podium was ripe for selling and very enticing to the two buyers. The Keys resort getaway symbolized me revisiting my past one last time before moving on for good.

However, I would not be made a fool. I buried any sentimentality, turning back to Elise and Bart. "I expect nothing but the best from both of you." My voice was sharp. "I've worked too damn hard to build this company. Don't screw this up."

Elise met my eyes unflinchingly. "Certainly, Mr. Harmon. I'll make sure everything goes perfectly."

Her calm poise balanced my intensity, and I was glad she was coordinating this trip. "Elise, call my pilot to secure the jet. Wheels up at eight a.m. tomorrow. Be at Teterboro Airport by seven forty-five." I turned to face my assistant fully. "I'm trusting you with the critical job of liaising between the resort staff and bidders. You'll join all our meetings and meals too. I expect you to be close by the entire time. Understood?"

Again, Elise's eyes briefly widened, but she quickly nodded. In three years as my assistant, she had almost never accompanied me on a business trip. But for this, I needed her organizational skills and attention to detail. She was a tool in my success, one I aimed to utilize to the fullest. "Of course. I'll get the jet scheduled immediately."

"Good. That will be all."

Elise stood and marched out of the room, her heels clicking on the marble floor. This trip would serve its purpose, an optimal backdrop for stimulating the bidders' competitiveness. I ignored the nostalgic pang the thought of Calypso Key provoked.

Sentiment was for fools.

I would orchestrate the perfect business arrangement, recharge my mind while scuba diving in the clear Caribbean Sea, then walk away even richer and more successful. Nothing would distract me from my goal. Not even the beautiful island paradise from my past. After all, other than a few exceptions, this trip was about business, not pleasure.

With everything in order, Bart and I discussed a few final points before I dismissed him. Alone again, I stared at the two offers, determination pulsing through my veins.

I STEPPED INTO MY SLEEK, modern Manhattan penthouse, the wall of windows showcasing the glittering cityscape. Crossing the open-concept living space, I headed into my bedroom and straight for the walk-in closet to pack.

I selected each item with care—several designer suits, a pair of Italian leather shoes, and a custom-tailored tuxedo, sure. But I also packed polo shirts, cargo shorts, swim trunks, and sport sandals. Mostly business, yes. But my brother had insisted I relax and enjoy myself at least a little.

As I set the suitcase by the door, my cell rang with Nate's face flashing on my home screen. My brother had been through a rough patch, but he came out of it stronger and with renewed purpose thanks to his new girlfriend, Camille Sullivan. Over the past few months, he'd turned his life around, forging ahead with a new career.

I tapped the button to answer. "Hey, little brother. What's up?"

"Oh, not much. You know, the biggest holiday of the year? How's everything going with the trip?"

I refused to rise to his Christmas jab. "Couldn't be

better. The jet's booked for tomorrow morning. You and Camille still planning to fly down?"

"Yeah, we'll be there before the big event. Don't worry. We've got a hockey camp starting tomorrow for Skate to Success, but it's only for two days. Thanks for setting everything up. I know you've got a lot on your plate."

"Of course. That's what I do."

"Yeah, I know. I'm looking forward to seeing Calypso Key again." His voice took on a dreamy tone, and I smiled. Nate and Camille had vetted the resort several months ago to ensure it would be the perfect setting for our gala. They had fallen in love in the process.

"So am I," I said as I poured a glass of single malt from the beverage station in a corner of my sitting area. "And I'm taking your advice and plan to mix a little pleasure in with my business."

"Oh?" His voice took on a speculative tone. "Looking to have a vacation fling?"

"Absolutely not," I said sharply. "Female distraction is the last thing I need right now. I was talking about doing some diving and sightseeing." I tried not to think about the Czech supermodel I'd broken up with last summer, after months of miserable dating.

"I can vouch for both. And I'm glad to hear it. You need to quit working yourself to death."

"In a few more days, it'll all be worth it," I replied quietly. "I'll see you in Florida."

After the call ended, I stared at the taillights of cars far below and shook my glass, listening to the light music of ice cubes rattling against the crystal tumbler. A grim smile rose on my face. Focused on my target, I was a heat-seeking missile. Nothing could move me off course.

Chapter Two

Elise

THE SKY outside my window was dark as I methodically packed my belongings inside my tiny Queens apartment. I glanced around the cozy space, taking in the neat shelves and cute decorations adorning the walls. It might not be much, but Clay Harmon paid me well enough that I could afford my own apartment without a roommate. A luxury in New York City that I didn't take for granted. And concentrating on my job distracted me from the fact that I'd had no real plans for Christmas, just a phone call to my parents. My mind replayed the day, which had been full of surprises.

After the meeting, Bart had swaggered by my desk, flashing a grin. "Big trip ahead, right? The Florida Keys will be paradise."

I forced a polite smile, still getting used to the idea that I was coming along. "Yes, it should be interesting."

"Interesting." Bart's eyes held mine a beat too long. "I look forward to it too. You and I have never gotten to spend much time together."

Thank God for the stack of documents on my desk. I busied myself organizing the files to avoid meeting his gaze. "Just focusing on the work, as always. Enjoy the rest of your Christmas."

Bart laughed and sauntered off, reeking of cheap cologne. I scowled, hoping I could avoid him during the trip as much as possible. That was the downer of the day. The high point had come as I was leaving the office, when I'd knocked on my boss's door with a quick rap of my knuckles.

"Come in."

He sat behind his desk, icy pale-blue eyes glued to his computer screen. Dark hair perfectly styled, even at the end of the day. His broad shoulders were rigid with tension, and a crease had formed between his brows. I cleared my throat. "Just wanted to see if you need anything else. I'll see you bright and early for our flight tomorrow."

His gaze never lifted from the screen before him. "That will be all. Good night, Elise." His tone was distant and preoccupied.

My cheeks flushed in frustration that he never saw me as a human being, even calling me into the office on Christmas Day. I did my best not to be irritated that he'd sprung this trip on me with almost no notice. Just assuming I'd be able to hop on his private jet at the snap of his fingers. Fortunately, knowing how important this trip to the Keys was and that there might be last-minute changes, I'd already cleared my schedule of outside conflicts.

I smiled politely. "Good night, Mr. Harmon."

Before I could back out of his office, he said, "It's Clay."

I blinked at him, my shock ten times that of being invited on the trip. "I'm sorry?"

Finally, he lifted his gaze. Something in my stomach fluttered when his eyes met mine. As much as he never saw me as anything but a piece of furniture, there was no denying my boss was a very gorgeous man. "Call me Clay. We've worked together for over three years now. It seems unnecessary to keep calling me Mr. Harmon, especially when we'll be traveling together."

My heart stuttered, and I moistened my lips. "O-of course. Good night... Clay." The word was like a foreign language on my tongue.

"See you tomorrow." He dropped his eyes back to his computer screen, dismissing me.

But still, I floated out of his office. It might have been a tiny gesture, but frozen robot Clay Harmon might have just thawed a little. I packed up all the necessary files and documents into three banker's boxes and pushed them out of Podium's offices using a handcart. A smile lingered on my lips at the thought of calling my boss by his first name. Was it possible that there was a different side to him? I smirked as I drove out of the parking garage.

Even if there is, it's not like he's going to show it to me. I'm just a minion, remember?

Turning back to packing, I crossed the room to my battered wooden dresser. I ignored my glasses laying on top —I only used them for computer work. Instead, I lifted a resin angel, less than four inches tall, from the scarred top, its chipped paint a familiar sight. I turned it over in my palm, the smooth coolness of the surface a comfort against my skin. A silent reminder, and one I needed with me. I carefully tucked the angel in the corner of my suitcase. It would keep me grounded amidst the opulence of Calypso Key.

I rolled up another blouse, placing it in my suitcase next to a one-piece swimsuit and a bikini. Unsure which to pack, I'd decided on both. As I continued packing, I couldn't shake the feeling that this trip was going to be more work than pleasure. Sure, I was excited about the invitation—it felt like a validation of my hard work and dedication. A floppy sensation rolled through my core again at the thought of visiting a tropical resort with Clay Harmon.

Too bad Bart had to come too. "Ugh, what a slimeball," I muttered under my breath, dreading the thought of spending time with Podium's gross CFO. But he was a necessary and inevitable part of the event.

"Elise, are you sure you don't want me to help you pack?" my best friend, Rachel, called from the living room. She'd insisted on coming over, claiming that she couldn't let me leave without a proper send-off, especially considering the holiday. She'd spent the morning and afternoon with her parents and brother.

"No, thanks," I called back, trying to sound cheerful. "I'm almost done."

"Okay, but if you change your mind, I'm right here," Rachel said, popping her head into my bedroom. Her dark, shoulder-length hair swished softly. My neighbor, she was one of the first people I'd met after moving to New York three years ago. Also twenty-nine, her breezy, casual nature balanced my driven ambition. As she leaned against the doorframe, her brown eyes scanned my suitcase, then met mine with a concerned expression. "Are you worried about Bart?"

"Not really," I said with a roll of my shoulder. "He might be overly familiar and kind of slimy, but he's like that with everyone."

"You need to treat this trip as a reward for all your accomplishments. Don't let him ruin it for you."

I inhaled deeply, trying to let her words sink in. "You're right. Thanks."

"Of course." She smiled, then it fell as she screwed one eye shut. "Do you really have to go scuba diving with him, though?"

I laughed and rubbed my forehead. "Yeah. Mr. Harmon thinks it's a team bonding exercise for us and insists on the three of us going. He informed us of that fact this afternoon." I smiled at the automatic use of his last name. *Gonna have to change that...* "I'll probably make a fool of myself."

"You'll do great! If anyone will be terrible at it, it'll be Bart." She shot me a grin and waggled her eyebrows. "On the plus side, you're probably going to get a nice view of the gorgeous and mysterious Clay Harmon shirtless."

I gave her a deadpan look, but my stomach skittered around my abdomen. His suits always fit his broad shoulders perfectly, so I could just imagine what lay underneath them.

She let the subject drop and instead sent me a sly smile. "So I guess you're not so mad at me anymore for dragging you to those scuba classes to be my buddy, huh?"

I paused with a pair of leggings in my hand, considering. "You're right. I might not have been terribly enthusiastic at the time, but I'm glad to be certified now. So thank you." I gave her a slight bow then placed the leggings in my luggage. Two months ago, she'd begged me to take scuba lessons with her, and I'd finally relented, juggling the several-week course with all my other obligations. But I had to admit that now I was looking forward to diving in warm, clear water. Our checkout had been in a cold, murky quarry.

"You're very welcome. Are you going to raid the Clay Harmon black card and stock up on designer clothes?" Rachel asked with another grin. "You know, take advantage of the billionaire budget?"

I snorted and shook my head as I added a sundress, perfect for the tropical climate. "I'd be the last person he'd ever offer it to, even if I was interested. Which I'm not. I'm there to work, remember? Not to play dress-up."

"Fine, fine." she held her hand up in mock surrender. "Elise Briggs, the ever-efficient executive assistant. You'll be back in those sensible suits before we know it."

I gave her a pointed look. "Exactly. He's depending on me to ensure everything proceeds without a hitch."

She gave me the look right back, not buying it. "He is kind of an ass, though. To just casually mention he expects you to tag along at the last minute. Plus making you work on Christmas! I guess he's not known for his sensitivity, though, is he?"

"No, he's not."

Her eyes became round. "Do you think he wants to have a fling with you? Is that why he invited you?"

A laugh tumbled out of my mouth as I tossed in a pair of shorts. "I don't think he has flings with anyone. He's too serious. And the man doesn't even view me as a human. Romance is the last thing on his mind."

"That's his loss, isn't it? You deserve someone who appreciates you." Rachel patted the side of the doorjamb. "Now finish up so we can have a glass of wine before you leave."

With renewed determination, I completed my packing and zipped up my suitcase. Despite my concerns about Bart, I couldn't deny the surge of excitement rising inside me for the trip. This was my chance to not only enjoy the beautiful tropical location but also to prove to Clay that I was more than just his invisible subordinate.

There, I was getting used to the first name!

I was very good at what I did, but I wanted to be more

than an executive assistant. And Clay Harmon's empire could provide endless opportunities.

As I prepared for bed, I set my suitcase by the door next to the banker's boxes. All was ready for tomorrow. My thoughts returned to Clay. He was magnetic, incredibly handsome, and terrifyingly intelligent. But he was also my boss, and not to mention way, way out of my league.

I'd arranged countless dinner dates and weekend trips for him with various women over the years, but none of those relationships lasted. I was never clear whether it was because of Clay's workaholic tendencies or something else entirely.

"Life isn't a fairy tale," I muttered to myself, acknowledging the truth that billionaire CEOs don't fall for their assistants in real life. It might make for a thrilling romance novel, but reality was much less glamorous. I needed to stay focused on my job and the opportunity this trip presented.

Tomorrow would be a new day, a new adventure. I vowed to keep a professional distance from my billionaire boss, no matter how blue those eyes were, or the power he exuded from every pore.

I woke before my alarm, too excited to sleep any longer. The thought of traveling on Clay's private jet added to the thrill. My two business trips with him had been in the city, and we'd traveled by car.

"This is going to be so different," I told myself as I stretched in bed, welcoming the day ahead.

After a shower, I set to work curling my hair and applying minimal makeup. I stared at my reflection, satisfied that I looked both professional and put together. Next, I dressed in a soft blue business suit and black pumps, figuring this was a business trip after all and wanting to present the proper image.

As if on cue, the buzzer sounded, announcing the arrival of the company driver. After wriggling my fingers to dispel the nerves, I wrangled my suitcase and the banker's boxes, neatly stacked them onto a handcart, and made my way down the elevator. The weight of the boxes felt symbolic of the responsibility I carried, both professionally and personally.

"Morning, Elise," the driver greeted me with a friendly smile as he opened the door to the car. "Ready for your trip?"

"Good morning, Fred. And yes, I'm more than ready," I replied, trying to sound confident despite the butterflies in my stomach.

"Great," Fred said cheerfully as he helped me load my luggage into the trunk. "Let's get you to Teterboro."

As we pulled away from my building, I exhaled through my nose, then looked for a distraction from my nerves. I'd never been to a private airport before. We exchanged Christmas pleasantries while he navigated the morning traffic, and I asked after his wife and son.

"They're doing great, thank you. My son just started soccer last week, and Tracy is busy with her book club." He nodded in the rearview mirror. "You always remember the little things."

I smiled fondly at him. Fred had worked for Podium for years and drove me whenever I needed to go somewhere for business. Clay might be an aloof figure himself, but he was a stickler for making sure his employees enjoyed a good working environment. Bart Mayhew was one of the few people I didn't care for.

Before I knew it, we'd arrived at Teterboro Airport. Anticipation filled me as Fred pulled up alongside a sleek white jet. This private airport was a world away from the bustling commercial terminals I was used to, and I didn't even need to clear security. I took a deep breath, trying to calm my pounding heart.

"Here we are," the driver announced, putting the car into park. "I'll take care of your luggage, and your ID has already been processed. You go right ahead and board the plane."

"Thanks for the ride, Fred."

Exiting the car, I gulped at the impressive aircraft before me. I'd never been near Clay's private Gulfstream jet. I felt like I was stepping into an entirely different world, one where anything could happen.

Climbing the steps to the entrance, I debated if the tropical destination might be enough to coax him out of his designer suits and into something more casual. I laughed quietly at the thought, shaking my head. I wouldn't be surprised if he slept in a suit. I reached the top of the staircase and stepped onboard. As soon as I entered the cabin, my gaze landed on Clay as he sat in an oversized cream-colored leather seat.

And he wasn't in formal business attire.

My billionaire boss was dressed in a light-blue Lacoste polo the exact same shade as his eyes and a pair of gray cargo shorts.

Shorts!

My gaze quickly took in a pair of muscular calves anchored in Italian leather loafers. His normally immaculately groomed hair was more natural today, and a section in the front had dropped onto his forehead. He absently brushed it back. My eyes widened, and I felt both over-dressed and a little embarrassed that I had misjudged him.

"Welcome aboard," he greeted me politely, his voice deep and cool. "Please have a seat. The flight attendant will bring you some coffee." He indicated the seat across the aisle from him.

"Thank you," I replied, trying to sound composed despite my disquiet. As I settled into the plush leather seat, Clay checked his Philippe Patek watch with a frown.

"Is everything okay?"

"Yes," he assured me. "Bart just called to say he's running late. We should be taking off shortly."

"Ah, I see," I said, nodding.

After I'd received my coffee and enjoyed half of the rich brew, the sound of footsteps climbing the jet's stairs caught my attention, signaling Bart's arrival. He stepped into view, wearing khakis paired with a plaid button-down shirt that had seen better days. His outfit was a far cry from Clay's effortlessly stylish look.

"Hey there, Elise!" Bart greeted me with an enthusiastic tone after exchanging more subdued hellos with Clay. He pleaded bad traffic for the delay.

I forced a smile. "Good morning, Bart."

As the CFO took a seat behind me, I glanced over at Clay, who had been engrossed in the *Wall Street Journal*. He carefully folded the paper, his brows lowered as he frowned at us. "Now that you're all here, let's go." Picking up a wall phone next to his seat, he notified someone, presumably the pilot, that we were ready to leave.

As the plane taxied down the runway, Bart leaned forward. "Your first private jet ride? I've been on plenty with Clay. Never gets old."

"Sure different than flying coach," I agreed, trying not

to grimace at the scent of bacon on his breath. I shifted away from him and tried to appear unfazed. I'd been on plenty of commercial flights, but this was a different world. One I'd never experienced. And one that I'd leave behind the moment we returned to New York. I decided to concentrate on the tasks awaiting me once we landed—verifying documents, attending meetings, and ensuring everything went smoothly for Podium's benefit.

Once we were airborne, I studied my surroundings more closely. The interior of the Gulfstream was something out of a movie. Gleaming wood paneling lined the walls, and buttery-soft cream leather seats were arranged in a spacious seating area. Two polished tables, crafted from some exotic wood, stood with the aisle separating them. The three of us sat in a separate section, with pairs of chairs in two rows. It was difficult to ignore the view of the city shrinking below, a miniature gray landscape of skyscrapers and winding streets.

"Can I offer you something to drink?" a young woman asked as she emerged from what I presumed was the galley. Her name tag read *Brenda*, and she was dressed in a smart black uniform with a crisp white scarf knotted at her neck.

"Coffee, please," I replied, trying to sound nonchalant and probably failing.

Brenda nodded and disappeared. Moments later, she returned with a silver tray, setting down a bone china cup and saucer. Next to it, she placed a delicate puff pastry dusted with powdered sugar.

The flight attendant soon reappeared, her expression alert. "Mr. Harmon, breakfast is ready whenever you are."

Clay nodded, closing his laptop. "Thank you, Brenda."

She gestured to a small table set up with white linen and silverware. "Please follow me."

We moved to the section with seats around the two tables, with Clay and Bart sitting side by side and me across from them. Brenda served us a breakfast of eggs Benedict, fresh fruit, and an unbelievable amount of cheeses and pastries. I watched as Clay casually took a bite of his eggs as he read the paper, like he ate meals this delicious every single day. I focused on my own plate, forcing myself to ignore the opulence surrounding us. This was Clay's world, but it sure wasn't mine.

As we ate, Bart continued to chatter about nothing of importance. I did my best to tune him out, thankful when he finally leaned back in his seat and closed his eyes. Within minutes, soft snores emanated from him.

Figures. Even when he's asleep, he can't keep his damn mouth shut.

As Clay darted a glance at Bart, a flash of irritation crossed his face before he schooled his features into a neutral mask. He pulled out his laptop and began typing, effectively shutting us both out. And that prompted me to work on my own tasks.

Unfortunately, the CFO woke up as soon as we began our descent. But that couldn't dampen my anticipation. When the plane touched down in Key West, I craned my face to look out the window, excited to face the undoubtedly challenging days ahead. As the exterior door opened, warm, humid air entered and caressed my skin, signaling we had left icy New York far behind.

But what lay ahead?

Chapter Three

Clay

AS I SHUT my briefcase and prepared to leave the jet, I glanced at Elise and Bart. Excitement was written on their faces as they craned their heads to look out the window. I was a little envious of their enthusiasm.

"The water is so many shades of blue!" Elise said as we climbed into the limousine she had arranged. Her dark-blue eyes sparkled, complementing the water behind her.

"Definitely not the Hudson River," I replied. My stomach tightened as our gazes met, which had never happened. I hardly ever spared her a second glance, and now I frowned.

Fortunately, distraction arrived in the form of an email on my phone. In addition to the Podium sale, my other major project at the moment was the acquisition of an electric vehicle technology company. I tapped out a quick reply, pleased the GreenDrive venture was progressing.

The forty-five-minute drive flew by, punctuated by long

stretches of highway soaring over nothing but ocean. Soon we found ourselves atop a gentle hill on the northern end of Calypso Key. The view was breathtaking. The Key's name-sake resort sprawled below us, hugged by the turquoise ocean that stretched out endlessly to the south. A wave of nostalgia washed over me, childhood memories flooding back as I took in the sight before me.

"Excellent," I murmured, inspecting the buildings as we neared the lobby and finding my adult standards met. Twinkling holiday lights, dim in the daylight, were strung under the eaves and more were wrapped around the trunks of nearby trees. "Nate told me they really stepped up their game, but seeing it in person is rather gratifying."

As our limo pulled to a stop in front of the one-story lobby building, my door was opened. After I exited, a thirtyish man shook my hand. He was about my height and wore a blue staff button-down shirt. His light-brown hair was short and neat.

"Welcome to Calypso Key Resort." He smiled warmly and shook our hands in turn before settling his gaze on me. "We're very pleased to see you back, Mr. Harmon. I'm Evan Markham, the general manager. I'll be your point of contact during your stay, and available for whatever you might need."

"Thank you. We appreciate it," I replied. Despite my preoccupations, I was gratified the manager himself was meeting us.

"Let's get you all settled in," Evan suggested, leading us farther into the resort. "We'll bypass the lobby, and I'll check you in directly."

As we walked, Evan favored his right leg slightly. "We recently underwent a major renovation," he explained, his blue eyes warm and friendly. "The resort is much more modern and luxurious than you might remember from your childhood, Mr. Harmon."

"I can see that," I said, glancing around. Everything was new—clean lines and natural wood accents blended seamlessly with the tropical setting. "It's quite impressive. Tropical and yet modern."

Evan smiled. "Thank you. Guest satisfaction is our top priority, and I want to assure you we will do everything possible to make your stay and the New Year's Eve gala a complete success." He tipped his head to Elise. "It's nice to finally meet you in person."

"Likewise! I feel like we're old friends after all our correspondence. Thank you for being so accommodating to my pestering these past few weeks." Elise laughed and her nose wrinkled, something else I'd never noticed before.

Why the hell am I thinking about her face?

The general manager grinned. "It was hardly pestering. I think we have everyone's requirements noted." He turned to me and inclined his head. "Elise has been a great help with planning."

Bart held his hand out to Evan, and they shook. "I'm the guy who makes sure the final bill gets paid," Bart added, and I had to work to keep from wincing.

"Uh, pretty sure that's Clay," Elise murmured. I couldn't help the small smile that rose on my face as our eyes held for a moment.

We arrived at a row of beachfront cottages standing above a long stretch of white powder. A light, warm breeze carried the scent of the ocean and rustled the palm fronds above.

"Here we are," Evan said, coming to a stop. "Yours is on

the end, Mr. Harmon. We've put you in a two-bedroom unit with a private pool. I should also mention that Ms. Rhodes and Mr. Dubois are in cottages farther down the beach." He gestured down the row of similar beachfront accommodations before turning back. "Ms. Briggs, Mr. Mayhew, your cottages are next door to Mr. Harmon's. Both are identical, with lovely views of the ocean."

Evan's eyes met mine briefly and he gave me a slight nod, confirming he'd come through regarding the request I'd made this morning before leaving New York. After our Christmas staff meeting, it had occurred to me that Elise hadn't planned on accompanying us on the trip. An unexpected hint of chagrin filled me. So while I was reading the paper on the jet, I'd phoned Evan personally and he assured me Elise had already called and was booked into a garden cottage. I asked if she could be upgraded, and obviously, Evan had made it happen. I nodded back.

He swept his gaze over the three of us. "Would you like me to show you each the features of your rooms?"

Bart looked like he was gearing up to accept, so I shook my head before he could make himself any more of an ass. "No, thank you. I'm sure we'll be quite comfortable." I was already envisioning an evening swim as the sun set over the water.

"Very well, Mr. Harmon." Evan nodded, handing each of us a keycard. "As per your request, I've arranged a private scuba diving trip for you three tomorrow morning. April will be your personal divemaster."

"I can't wait!" Elise's eyes lit up with excitement as she glanced at me. Their deep-blue color reminded me of a velvet twilight sky. Which was another weird thought. I focused on her words as she continued. "I only got certified a month ago. I can't wait to explore the underwater world here."

Bart chimed in, somewhat defensively, "I've been certified for years. Haven't dived in a while, though. I'm sure it's like riding a bike."

I remained silent, not wanting to boast or downplay their enthusiasm. I had been certified for years as well, but I took a refresher course a week ago to ensure I was adequately prepared for any challenges we might find beneath the waves.

Elise's infectious excitement was endearing, and I found myself looking forward to sharing this experience with her. An image of her in a string bikini flashed into my mind and I felt like slapping myself.

Get a grip, idiot! She's your assistant, remember?

"I'm sure you'll both do fine," Evan said, his warmth evident in his smile. "April is an exceptional divemaster, and she'll make sure you all have a safe and enjoyable time. If there's anything else you need during your stay, don't hesitate to contact me directly." He handed us each a business card.

"Thank you, Evan," I responded, shaking his hand firmly. As he took his leave, I noticed his slight limp once again. A reminder that even in paradise, life had its trials.

***

AFTER SETTLING INTO MY COTTAGE, which more than met my needs, our little trio met for lunch. As I took my seat at the wooden table of the resort's casual dining restaurant, Dorado, sunlight glittered on the surface of the nearby free-form pool. A decorated Christmas tree with wrapped presents underneath stood in one corner. Elise slid into a chair across from me, the light bringing out hints of honey and cinnamon in her hair. She'd traded her business suit for a breezy pink sundress that bared her slender shoulders and collarbones. I caught myself staring at the hollow of her throat and quickly lifted my eyes.

Bart dropped into the chair beside me with a grunt and grabbed his menu. "I'm starving. I wonder what's good here. I gotta say, this place sure beats the cold courtroom back home. My soon-to-be ex-wife is putting me through the wringer."

The last thing I wanted to do was discuss Bart's marital problems, so I asked Elise the first thing that popped into my head. "I hope your family life is more enjoyable than Bart's."

She blinked in surprise, like she couldn't believe I'd asked. "Oh, uh, my parents are still back in Millbrook, where I grew up. No boyfriend or anything."

I noticed the *no boyfriend* comment, though I kept my face expressionless. In truth, I was rather nonplussed to realize that I knew almost nothing about her. After three years of working together. Then she smiled, and my eyes focused on her face. Had that little dimple in her cheek always been there?

"I grew up in a small town in Pennsylvania, but I've always yearned for the big city," she continued. "So I've had the best of both worlds."

After ordering, we settled into conversation. It was a new dynamic for us, less strained and formal. Even Bart became less smarmy, and Elise stopped scooting her chair away from him.

After lunch, I headed down the beach to check on Podium's two top bidders. Both were in their fifties. Laurent

Dubois answered the door in a silk robe, polite but standoff-ish. Though dressed casually, his trimmed salt-and-pepper hair was neatly styled. He insisted he didn't need a thing.

Several cottages down the beach, Celeste Rhodes was much warmer, exclaiming about the beautiful cottage and thanking me for the special treatment. Her ash-blonde hair was cut to her shoulders and her loose pants and white blouse were both professional and suitable for the warm climate. I invited both on tomorrow's diving excursion, but Laurent looked mortified that I'd even suggest it. Celeste politely declined, citing a preference for beach time.

With formalities and welcomes completed, I headed back. The minute I was back in my cottage, I changed into board shorts. The cool water of my private pool felt amazing on my skin after the island heat. Though my pool had an expansive view of the beach and ocean, the cottage's location at the far eastern end ensured privacy. I sank down until just my head was above the surface, leaning back and closing my eyes.

When I'd had enough and was toweling off, tomorrow's dive played through my mind. I could already picture the swaying sea fans and schools of tropical fish. I smiled to myself, cracking open a local craft beer that I retrieved from the minifridge in my living room. With a sigh, I sat at the table on my pool deck. The cold brew was crisp and bright, with hints of citrus. It perfectly complemented the warm breeze drifting in off the sea.

This getaway might be just what I needed. I couldn't wait to get in the water tomorrow. Out here, it felt like the rest of the world barely existed.

But it did exist.

And as the sun dipped lower in the sky, I turned my mind to our welcome reception in an hour. Time to get ready. As I slipped back inside my bedroom, an errant thought flitted through my brain. What might Elise wear tonight... Business attire like this morning or a breezy dress like this afternoon? A smile raised my lips. Alone inside my cottage, I could indulge in the forbidden fancy. After all, I'd never act on it.

Chapter Four

Elise

I FINISHED UNPACKING, placing the last of my clothes in the dresser drawers and setting my toiletries on the bathroom counter. My gaze swept around the modern, airy bathroom with its gray stone counter and white tiled walk-in shower. I certainly couldn't fault the accommodations. I changed into comfortable leggings and a tank top, relieved to be out of my constricting business suit, then padded into the large, main room.

My cottage was gorgeous. When I'd spoken to Evan prior to the trip, he found me a garden cottage, their simplest accommodations. And I was grateful to get that with so little notice, yet I ended up in a room with a stunning ocean view. I suspected Clay had upgraded me—Evan hadn't said anything about a choice in rooms. The thought caused my stomach to do a quiet little flip-flop.

Despite the calming view and the plush surroundings of my cottage, I couldn't shake the restless energy humming through my body now that I was actually here. The white walls and warm wood floors of the spacious room did little to soothe me. I grinned at my little angel, safe and sound on my nightstand. A king-sized bed with a white striped comforter and an abundance of pillows in soothing blues and greens sat in the back corner of the room, but sleep was the last thing on my mind.

I paced back and forth, my bare feet silent against the cool wooden floor. The three banker's boxes of documents were neatly arranged in the corner and my eye kept landing on them. The enormity of the task ahead, helping organize the sale of Podium and the upcoming New Year's Eve gala, felt like a physical weight on my back. My carefully crafted to-do list for the next few days was already three pages long.

I glanced at my phone, noting the time. Less than four hours until the cocktail reception to welcome our potential buyers. I headed for the sliding door that led to my private deck overlooking the ocean. I needed fresh air. Now.

Stepping outside, the warmth of the late afternoon sun embraced me. The gentle sea breeze carried the scent of salt air and blooming plumeria, a sweet, exotic fragrance that did little to ease the tension knotting my shoulders.

I set off on a walk, following a winding path that meandered through the resort. The carefully manicured lawns and swaying palm trees were a picture of tropical paradise, a stark contrast to the wintery streets I'd left behind in New York. As I rounded a bend in the path, I spotted an elegant man seated at a table near the pool bar. A young woman, dressed in a revealing sundress, draped herself across him, her expression haughty and bored.

I recognized him instantly. Laurent Dubois was one of the two potential buyers for Podium. I'd studied his photo during my meticulous internet research, making a note of his sharp jawline and the arrogant glint in his eye. Seeing him in person, I found my initial assessment confirmed.

He shook his empty glass as a server approached them. Laurent barely acknowledged the young man, his mouth curled with disdain as he snapped his fingers impatiently. "Another round," he demanded, his tone clipped and condescending despite his elegant French accent. Irritation surged through me on the server's behalf, along with a growing unease about the upcoming negotiations. Laurent was clearly a man accustomed to getting his own way.

And I'm going to have to deal with him directly. Oh, goody.

And that encounter was only a few hours away. I left the couple to their drinks. As I continued my walk, I rounded a bend in the path and came across a standalone building. A sign with flowing script read, *Calypso Calm*. The entrance was a small, covered porch with wooden benches and hanging baskets overflowing with exotic tropical flowers. It exuded a welcoming, peaceful vibe, and I was drawn toward it.

Through the large windows, I glimpsed a spacious room with a polished wooden floor. A comfortable seating area with a loveseat and several armchairs was arranged in one corner, while to the side, I glimpsed a larger room with a wall of mirrors. A small, trickling fountain added to the serene atmosphere. Large windows looked out to the swaying palm trees and the glittering ocean beyond.

Without thinking about it, I pushed open the door and stepped inside, inhaling the cool, fragrant air. The scent of essential oils mingled with the gentle sound of trickling water. A woman with warm brown eyes and a lovely smile greeted me from behind a sleek white counter. Her dark, curly hair was gathered into a loose bun at the nape of her neck. She wore black yoga pants and a fitted tank top that read *Lose Your Worries at Sandpiper Cay.*

"Hello there! Welcome to Calypso Calm," she said. "I'm Monica, the instructor. Are you interested in joining a class?"

My tension eased a little in her presence, and I glanced around the tranquil space. "I've never done yoga before. I was just curious."

"It's never too late to try something new," Monica encouraged. "I'm starting a restorative yoga class in just a few minutes. It's perfect for beginners, and a great way to unwind and de-stress. You could probably use a little of both, right?"

Her perceptive comment was right on. "That's tempting, but..." I hesitated, my gaze drifting to the open doorway of the studio. A handful of people were already settling onto their mats. They seemed so comfortable, so at ease. It was a foreign concept to me.

"It's okay to be unsure," she said, her voice soft and reassuring. "Yoga is about finding a connection with your body and breath, not about being perfect. Especially restorative yoga."

I was drawn to her calm, approachable manner—especially after witnessing Laurent's arrogant dismissiveness. But as I glanced around the tranquil space, my practical side reasserted itself. A wave of guilt washed over me. Here I was, exploring this luxurious island, indulging in frivolous thoughts of yoga while my to-do list stretched a mile long. And luxuries were something I'd never been comfortable with. The irony of enjoying Clay's lavish generosity, while feeling the pressure to prove my worth to him, settled in my stomach like a lead ball.

"It's more that I hadn't planned this. I have a lot to do before an event tonight."

"Of course." Monica's gaze softened, and she tilted her head slightly. "What time is this important event?"

"Seven o'clock," I admitted, my fingers toying with the waistband of my leggings.

"And it's now almost four." she pointed out gently. "You could easily spare an hour to de-stress, and still have plenty of time to get ready."

I opened my mouth to protest, but her words hit a nerve. She was right. I was clinging to my checklist like a life raft, but perhaps I needed a different kind of rescue. Maybe an hour of quiet reflection would be more valuable than another hour hunched over spreadsheets and contracts.

So I agreed to join the class since I was already wearing suitable clothing. Monica led me into the spacious studio, where a handful of other guests were preparing for the class. Soft music played in the background, adding to the soothing atmosphere. I was a little self-conscious at first, my movements stiff and uncertain as we began with gentle warm-up stretches.

Soon, however, my anxieties began to recede as Monica guided us through a series of restorative poses. We moved into a supported child's pose, my forehead resting on a soft block and my arms stretched out in front of me. A sense of calm washed over me as I focused on my breath, releasing the tension I'd been carrying in my shoulders and back. I even managed a supported bridge pose, my hips lifted and resting on a block, opening my chest and easing the tightness that seemed to have taken up residence in my lungs.

Throughout the session, my mind drifted back to Clay. To the man I'd seen on the plane earlier that day. Yet even in casual attire, he exuded an air of effortless sophistication.

And that lock of hair that kept falling onto his forehead... I sighed. There was something undeniably appealing about Casual Clay. He was different than the boss I saw at the office every day. Not necessarily more approachable, but... less intimidating. Perhaps the tropical air was affecting him too.

After class, I helped Monica put the mats away, maybe a little residual guilt seeping back in at enjoying myself. At the same time, the peaceful atmosphere, with its lingering scent of lavender and eucalyptus, made me reluctant to leave.

"You did great for your first class," she said, her warm, genuine smile like a soft blanket. "You seem to have a natural ability to connect with the poses."

"Thank you," I replied, surprised by how relaxed and refreshed I felt. "It was actually easier than I expected."

"Yoga can be surprisingly accessible," she said. "It's about finding what feels good for your body, not about forcing yourself into impossible positions."

"I'll keep that in mind." I hesitated for a moment, unsure how much to reveal. "I'm actually here on business. There's a very important event I need to make sure goes smoothly."

"It sounds like you have a lot on your plate," Monica observed, her brown eyes filled with understanding. "A little downtime now and again might be just what you need to stay focused."

I hesitated. A part of me agreed with her—I could already feel the tension creeping back into my shoulders as I thought about the reception. But old habits died hard.

"I'll be fine," I said, trying to convince myself as much as her. "I'm used to working under pressure."

"I admire your dedication," Monica said, her smile

unwavering. "But remember, taking care of yourself is just as important as taking care of business." She glanced at the clock on the wall. "I teach classes every day. Come back whenever you need a break. You're welcome anytime."

I smiled, touched by her offer. "Thank you. I'll keep that in mind." I glanced at my watch. It was just after five. "But I should probably get ready for the reception now."

"Of course," she said, her voice soothing. "Enjoy the evening."

"Thank you. I will. And thank you for the class. You were right—I feel recharged now."

As I left Calypso Calm, I felt lighter, both physically and mentally. Monica's words echoed in my mind: *Taking care of yourself is just as important as taking care of business.*

Maybe, but being here right now, an essential part of Clay's plans, had to be my top priority. If I'd learned anything in my twenty-nine years, it was that opportunities were fleeting and rare. And I'd worked too damn hard and suffered too much to let this one slip away.

Chapter Five

Clay

I ADJUSTED the knot of my silk tie, the vibrant aqua a stark contrast to the crisp white of my custom-tailored Zegna shirt. And I liked the subtle nod the tie gave to my surroundings. My gaze drifted toward the sliding glass door, where the landscaping lights glinted off the surface of my private pool. It had been less than an hour since I'd emerged from those cool, turquoise depths, and it had been just what I needed. Especially after discovering it was long enough for swimming laps.

I turned from the window to survey the living room of my two-bedroom cottage. The spacious room was a harmonious blend of modern elegance and tropical charm. White walls and polished wood floors created a sense of airiness, while the pale-blue sectional sofa and oversized armchairs invited relaxation. A vase overflowing with fresh tropical flowers sat on the coffee table, filling the air with a subtle fragrance. A solid wood dining table and chairs sat to one side of the area. Large sliding doors opened onto the private patio with an expansive ocean view, but right now my focus was on the task at hand.

I ran a hand over my neatly styled hair, the strands already drying into their usual precise order. Despite the long day, my reflection in the full-length mirror was the picture of a successful CEO—confident, powerful, and ready to conquer the world.

The insistent buzzing of my phone interrupted my moment of self-assessment. I ignored it for a moment, savoring the luxurious quiet of the cottage. But the buzzing persisted, an insistent demand for my attention. I sighed, my brief respite over.

I crossed the room and snatched the phone from the side table, glancing at the screen. Nate. Of course. "Good evening," I answered, my tone brisk and professional. "What's up?"

"Just checking in with you, big brother." As Nate's voice sounded through the speaker, a wave of warmth washed over me. "Everyone arrive okay? You all settled in?"

"Yes, everything is fine," I assured him as I settled onto the couch and stretched out my legs. "Bart, Elise, and I are in our respective cottages, and so are our two bidders. I have to admit, you were spot on about Calypso Key. The resort is impressive. You and Camille did a good job vetting it."

"Damn right we did." His voice held a dash of mischief I recognized instantly. He and Camille had done quite a bit more than vetting on their trip to the resort a few months ago. "Just trying to ensure you have an appropriate back drop for conducting the biggest deal of your life. And to make sure my final official duty as front man for Podium goes smoothly."

Younger than me by two years, my brother had been one of the most successful players in the NHL before a career-ending injury sent him into a tailspin he'd only recently dug himself out of. And his role as chief public relations officer for Podium had also been in jeopardy, but that was all in the past now.

"Don't worry," I reassured him, unable to keep a touch of pride from entering my voice. "I'm on top of my game. Every detail is planned to perfection."

He paused for a beat before continuing, his tone shifting to one of gentle concern. "Don't forget to take some time to relax, Clay. Even workaholics need a break once in a while, especially in paradise."

"Nate," I said, my voice taking on a sharper edge. "This is not a vacation. This is the most important business trip of our lives."

He sighed. "Ease up. I understand—Podium is our baby, and especially yours. You've worked like hell to make it a success." His voice softened. "But you're starting to sound like one of our investors."

"I did swim in my pool earlier. Is that sufficient relaxation for you?"

I could practically hear his eyeroll. "Oh, stuff it. No, a ten minute lap swim—which is what I'm sure you did—isn't what I had in mind. There's no need to be all business, no joy."

I scowled that he'd pegged me so well. I poured a glass of Macallan whisky from the bottle sitting on the coffee table. The resort had left the bottle in my room as a welcome gift. As I lifted it, swirling, the amber liquid caught the light, releasing a smoky, seductive scent. "I don't need joy. I need to succeed."

"You will succeed," he said, his usual light tone turning serious. "You always do. Doesn't mean you need to drive yourself into the ground in the process."

I softened a little. My brother always knew how to push my buttons, but he was also my biggest supporter. I took a sip of the Macallan, the smooth, peaty whisky warming my throat. "I'll find a way to take a break or two. Do some exploring."

"Need me to fly down early to make sure you actually do it?" he asked, a teasing lilt in his voice.

"No. I don't need a babysitter," I snapped back, but a whisper of a smile tugged at my lips.

"Just looking out for you, brother."

"Of course you are," I said, my tone mellowing. "But I've got this under control."

"Uh-huh," he said, unconvinced. "So what's on the agenda for the next few days besides wooing our buyers?"

Ha! This should please him. "I've arranged a private scuba diving excursion for tomorrow morning. Bart and Elise are joining me."

A stunned silence crackled through the phone line. Then Nate burst out laughing, the sound loud and echoing in the quiet of my cottage. "Seriously? You're taking Elise and Bart diving? Great, an excursion with your assistant and our monumental asshole of a CFO! Your idea of down-time leaves something to be desired, brother."

I silently agreed with his assessment of Bart but remained silent on the matter. "I want to ensure my team has an opportunity to enjoy themselves. A little team bonding never hurts."

"Team bonding, huh?" Nate's laughter subsided into a low chuckle. "Let me guess, you'll be discussing quarterly reports and profit margins on the dive boat?"

"We might," I said dryly. "Unless Elise manages to distract us with a SWOT analysis of the dive operator's competitive landscape."

"Ouch," Nate replied, a wince clear in his voice. "I'm surprised you even included her."

"She's an employee," I said, a touch of defensiveness creeping into my voice. "And part of the team."

"Right," Nate said slowly. "A gear in the machine."

I frowned, and my arm froze with the glass of whisky halfway to my mouth. "What are you trying to say, Nate?"

He sighed. "Maybe you should view the people who work for you as, you know, human beings. Not just pieces on a chessboard."

"What the hell is that supposed to mean? Elise hasn't used her dive certification yet, so I figured she'd enjoy the experience. And I'm including Bart too."

"It means you can be a real asshole."

"Oh, shut up!" I snapped. "I'm paying for them to enjoy a lavish tropical getaway, complete with gourmet meals and side excursions. I even upgraded Elise to a beachfront cottage, for God's sake."

A long beat of silence followed. "Oh, so she's right next door to you, huh?" A knowing amusement crept into Nate's voice.

My face flushed, and I frowned, unaccountably flustered. "The decision was entirely logical. Elise has been working nonstop on this deal. It was simply a way to acknowledge her hard work and dedication."

"And that's all it was? Just... acknowledgement?"

Confusion, followed by a flash of irritation, coursed through me. "What else would it be? She's my assistant, Nate, not my girlfriend."

"Haven't had one of those in a while, have you?"

"No. Because I've been working on the biggest deal of our lives. Remember?"

"Uh-huh. And now we're back to the fact that you seriously need to loosen up and enjoy yourself a little. And stop treating people like they're disposable."

"The three of us are going *diving* tomorrow. In crystal clear, tropical water. Does that sound like I'm a tyrant?"

"Oh yeah, you're a real soft touch, Clay," he replied, a grin lacing his voice. "I bet hanging out with their billionaire, driven boss is exactly what Bart and Elise have in mind when they think about enjoying themselves. Living the dream, man."

Despite myself, I burst out laughing and all my irritation dissolved. "You're such a dick, Nate."

"That's why you love me," he replied with a laugh. "I keep it real, whether you like it or not. Listen, I've got to run. Camille is waving a running shoe at me, and I bailed on our last run. So I've got no excuse this time. We'll see you in a few days. Enjoy yourself tomorrow, okay?"

"I will. Enjoy your run," I said, already picturing Camille's stately but slightly rundown Connecticut farmhouse that stood next to our childhood home. Despite Nate's self-deprecation, his blown-out knee was healing well, and he could outrun me any day of the week without even trying. "See you both soon."

I ended the call, and the warmth of our exchange faded, leaving a familiar sharp edge in its wake. As I set the phone down on the side table, my smile vanished. I rose and approached the mirror, adjusting my cuffs and smoothing my suit jacket. Gone was the playful brother, replaced by the man who built a multi-billion-dollar empire.

I was Clay Harmon, CEO of Podium, which was only a part of Harmon Enterprises. And I was ready for battle.

Chapter Six

Elise

THE PRIVATE DINING room at Orchid Restaurant hummed as I circulated, the room bustling with energy and laughter. I scanned the small crowd, taking in our two bidders with their entourages mingling amidst the soft clinking of wine glasses. My eyes landed on Clay, back to looking every bit the CEO in his black custom suit. Except tonight he'd added a tropical hint with a turquoise tie. The errant lock of hair was again suitably tamed as he held a glass of Cabernet in one hand. I didn't need to make any comparisons. He was easily the best-looking man in the room.

Clay had an effortless way of commanding attention, a magnetism that drew people in. My own outfit, a white blouse, tailored gray skirt, and black pumps, felt simple by comparison, but it would do for the professional image I wanted to maintain.

As I sipped my dry Riesling, I reflected on my surroundings. Our private venue for tonight was gorgeous. Partially open to the warm air, the heavenly scent of nearby colorful orchids drifted throughout. An open bar sat in the corner and two tables of gourmet hors d'oeuvres stretched along one wall.

"Your cottage looks lovely," said Sophie, Laurent's assistant, as she joined me. Also dressed for work, she held something fruity and tropical in one hand. "Lucky you. I'm sharing a garden bungalow with another of Laurent's hangers-on."

My smile was polite and professional. "I believe all the accommodations here are quite spectacular."

"Speaking of spectacular..." Celeste's assistant, Isabelle, sidled up next to us, her gaze fixed on Clay. "I've seen plenty of pictures in magazines, but he's even better looking in person, isn't he?" She twirled a strand of her curly golden hair, eyeing him like a perfectly cooked steak.

I swallowed the sudden pang that twisted in my stomach. Clay might be a robotic workaholic, but that didn't mean I liked seeing him viewed like he was on the menu. I inhaled, striving to be professional and forced a smile. "I couldn't say. I only view him as my boss."

Sophie smirked and raised her glass. "To breathtaking views, then. Both inside and outside our cottages."

I clinked my glass with hers and Isabelle's, then took a sip of wine. Once again, my eyes drifted to Clay as he spoke with Laurent.

As the evening progressed, I made a point to be ever the professional while conversing with both parties, trying to anticipate any need they might have. But I couldn't keep from sneaking glances at Clay. At his aqua-hued tie and the way it brought out the intensity of his eyes. Wrenching my gaze away, I concentrated instead on the western horizon, which still held a touch of crimson.

Catching movement, I steeled myself as Laurent sauntered toward me, his hair gleaming like polished silver and onyx.

"Ah, *bonsoir*," he drawled, his French accent dripping with disdain. "I must say, this little soirée is quaint, but my accommodations leave much to be desired."

Of course they do.

I bit the inside of my cheek, willing myself to maintain a placid expression. "I'm sorry to hear that, Mr. Dubois. Is there a particular issue with your beachfront cottage?"

Laurent's perfectly manicured hand waved dismissively. The gorgeous young woman clinging to his arm huffed a bored sigh, and she looked at least half his wife's age—his wife, who was nowhere to be found. I'd heard their marriage was rocky.

"It's all so... pedestrian," he continued. "I expected something more befitting a man of my stature."

The urge to throttle him surged through me, but I pushed it down and plastered on a solicitous smile. "I understand, sir. Perhaps I could speak with Evan Markham, the general manager? I'm sure he'd be more than happy to provide any additional amenities you might need to enhance your comfort."

"Additional amenities?" Laurent scoffed, his steel-blue eyes narrowing. "Ma chère, it would take a complete overhaul to bring that cottage up to par."

I tilted my head and maintained my mask. "If you have any specific concerns, Mr. Dubois, I'd be more than happy to discuss them with Evan myself. Your satisfaction is our utmost priority."

"I'm thirsty," the woman on his arm said in a thick eastern European accent, and waved her empty wine glass.

Laurent's gaze raked over me, a smirk playing at the

corners of his mouth. For a moment, I thought he might actually deign to provide details. Instead, he sniffed, swirling the dregs of champagne in his flute.

"I suppose it's too much to expect true luxury in this... antique place." He sighed dramatically. With a pointed look at his glass, he added, "Now, if you'll excuse me, we're in desperate need of a refill. At least the champagne is passable. French, of course."

As the pair sauntered away, I allowed myself a brief moment to close my eyes, exhaling slowly. When I opened them, my professional mask was back in place, ready to navigate the next challenge.

In contrast, Celeste was a delight. She was here unaccompanied, her husband having remained at their home in California. Her warm smile and genuine interest in Podium made her easy to talk to. She and her father, who still sat on the board of directors, built their company from nothing. As we discussed the upcoming schedule of events, I was confident that things were off to a great start, despite the disdainful Frenchman. Even Bart was making the rounds and being both helpful and gracious. To my surprise, I found myself getting along with him, even laughing a few times. Perhaps he wouldn't be as bad as I'd feared.

After the reception wound down, I retreated to my beautiful cottage, still touched by Clay's unexpected gesture. After a long, blissful shower, I poured myself a glass of cucumber infused water and stepped out onto the deck overlooking the beach and ocean. The starry darkness amplified the sound of waves lapping against the shore, and I eased out a long sigh, letting the soothing melody calm my nerves after the hectic day.

Clay's cottage was to my left, its windows glowing with soft interior light. I wondered if the lights were due to the turndown service or if he had left the reception. I took another sip of water, my thoughts drifting to tomorrow morning's diving excursion.

Closing my eyes, I allowed the peaceful sounds of the ocean to wash over me, my anticipation for the adventures ahead growing stronger with every moment.

THE NEXT MORNING, Clay, Bart, and I gathered on the deck next to the canal at the eastern edge of Calypso Key, preparing to board the boat *Indigo Heaven* for our private dive trip. I hadn't needed much time to choose my outfit, going with a sporty one-piece swimsuit and a white cover-up. I wasn't about to wear the red bikini I'd brought and bit back a laugh as I shook my head.

What possessed me to bring that?

As we approached the vessel tied up in the canal, April, our divemaster, greeted us with a warm smile. Wearing a long-sleeved rash guard and board shorts, her honey-blonde hair was plaited into two long braids.

"Good morning, guys!" she said. "I'm so excited to share this diving experience with you."

"Us too," I replied as my heart thumped steadily. Whether from nerves or excitement, I wasn't quite sure. "I can't wait to see what lies beneath these beautiful waters."

After we climbed aboard the boat, April went over safety procedures and equipment checks. I glanced at Clay, who was listening intently. When we'd met up, seeing him in a blue T-shirt and board shorts had made me do a double take. It was a little unsettling to realize there were facets to him that I was completely unaware of, that maybe there was more to the man than I'd given him credit for.

But that surprise was nothing compared to the shock I got when we neared the dive site, and April told us to start getting ready. Completely nonchalant, Clay pulled his T-shirt off and tossed it in the dry area, revealing a sculpted chest and muscular shoulders. His skin was pale, but he obviously spent plenty of time in the gym. I damn near gasped. Quickly, I focused my attention back on April, hoping no one had noticed my brief lapse in concentration.

Once we were suited up and briefed, we eagerly jumped off the stern platform and descended into the crystal-clear water. I was clumsy at first, considering this was my first dive post-certification.

But soon I forgot about being self-conscious.

The underwater world that revealed itself before us was nothing short of magical—vibrant coral formations and schools of colorful fish darting about. I fumbled with the unfamiliar gear, but April's steady presence helped me find my footing. Or rather, my swimming. When I gave her an affirmative nod that I was okay on my own, she took the lead of our little quartet. Clay eased closer to my side, remaining there throughout the dive.

He helped me several times when I fumbled with my bulky, vest-like buoyancy compensation device, providing assistance without ever being too forward. His silent concern touched me, even as I tried not to focus on how his pale eyes seemed even more vivid behind his mask. Instead, I allowed myself to become fully immersed in the wonders surrounding us.

We explored hidden nooks and crannies, admired the delicate dance of pale-pink sea anemones swaying in the gentle surge. We even spotted a shy reef shark in the distance. Bart looked even clumsier than I felt, and April had to help him several times as he became either too deep or too shallow.

In contrast, Clay's movements underwater were graceful and effortless. He seemed so connected with the environment around us, gliding through the water while maintaining a respectful distance from the delicate marine life.

Bart tugged on my arm, interrupting my musings. My flash of irritation at him fled when I followed his pointing finger with my eyes. A stunning red sea fan stood nearby, its intricate web of branches reaching out like a natural work of art. A pair of yellow-and-black butterfly fish nestled near the base. As Bart let go, his fingers brushed over my hand, lingering just a moment too long and distracting me from the fan's beauty. I yanked my hand away and swam back toward Clay and April, resisting the urge to scrub my skin.

Eventually, our dive came to an end, and we resurfaced, climbing back aboard *Indigo Heaven*. The sun was warm on our faces as we removed our gear and exchanged stories of our favorite discoveries.

"April, thank you for an incredible experience," Clay said with a smile, his voice full of warmth and so different from his business persona. This Casual Clay was like meeting a totally new person, someone I wanted to know better.

In contrast, Bart's behavior toward me swung back to being overly familiar, making me rethink last night's assessment at the reception that I'd misjudged him. He leaned in a bit too close as he spoke, his hand barely brushing against my shoulder. I shifted uncomfortably, unsure how to address the situation.

But before I could say anything, Clay commented, "Bart, despite the surroundings, we're professionals on a business trip. Let's act accordingly." His tone was deceptively light, but an unmistakable edge of steel lay beneath it.

Relief flooded through me, and some of the tension dissolved from my shoulders. I caught Clay's eye, and he gave me a deliberate nod.

Bart blinked, affecting an air of innocent confusion. "What do you mean? I was just being friendly."

Clay's eyes narrowed slightly. "I think you know exactly what I mean. Elise is a valued member of our team, so maintain a professional distance. Are we clear?"

Bart's face flushed red. "Crystal," he muttered, taking a step back as he turned to me. "I didn't mean anything by it. Sorry."

As Bart retreated to the other side of the boat, a rush of gratitude filled me. Not only had Clay noticed my discomfort, but he'd also taken action to address it. Just like that, I could breathe easily again, my focus returning to the beautiful ocean stretching out before us as we neared the canal to tie up to the dock.

Bart gathered his things and pleaded the need for a shower.

"I trust we'll see you at our strategy meeting at four this afternoon?" Clay asked.

"I'll be there," Bart replied. "It's a business trip, right? Gotta mix some work in with the fun." He headed toward his cottage, leaving Clay and me alone on the boat's deck. I inhaled, filling my lungs with the salty sea air.

Then I turned to face him. "I just wanted to say thank you for inviting me on this trip." His eyes met mine, their blue hue drawing me in. "It's been an amazing experience. I've never been anywhere tropical before."

When he smiled, a slight dimple appeared on one cheek. "You're welcome. I'm glad you're enjoying it."

"I'm guessing you had something to do with my gorgeous beach cottage. I distinctly remember booking a garden bungalow for myself."

His smile widened, and it was slightly sly. "Can't have our two bidders thinking I'm cheap now, can we?" Then he shrugged. "Besides, Podium can afford it."

"Thank you." I hesitated for a moment, searching for the right words. "I also appreciate how you handled Bart earlier," I added, my voice soft.

"Of course," he replied, his gaze sharpening. "I want everyone on our team to feel comfortable and respected. Has he crossed any lines with you?"

I hesitated, but I honestly couldn't say yes. "He hasn't. But it never hurts to have the boss throw in a word."

He eyed me evenly, as if he sensed I was holding back. "I won't tolerate harassment. Of anyone. If he makes you uncomfortable, tell me. I'll take care of it."

The last thing I wanted was to appear as a weak woman who needed protecting, so I waved him off. "That won't be necessary. I can handle myself."

"Yes, I've noticed that," he said quietly. Again, our eyes held, and a ripple traveled slowly, deliciously, down my body.

I tore my gaze away to stare at the scuba tanks. "You dive very well. How long have you been certified?"

He paused, and his gaze drifted into the distance. "I've loved the ocean as long as I can remember. I think that's why I recall our vacations here so vividly. I got certified in college as part of a class. Nate and I went on a trip together to the Maldives about eight years ago, but holidays have been few and far between for me."

I nodded, studying him as he revealed yet another layer to the man under the suit. I had no idea he'd gone on vacations with his brother. Though their destination of the luxurious island nation once more brought home the gulf between us. "I'm an only child. It's nice that you have such a close relationship with your brother."

"We've had our disagreements, but we've always been close. After he had to leave the NHL, I was really concerned about him. I'm pleased he's on the right path now."

I'd had many conversations with Nate over the past few years, most of them when he called Clay's office line, which went through me. The two men were very different, with Nate being friendly and affable. In direct opposition to Clay's formal, aloof intimidation.

Except that man seemed a world away right now.

As we left the boat, he subtly slipped April a tip, and I knew from experience that he was always generous in expressing his appreciation. It was a classy gesture and not lost on me. As Clay and I walked toward the beach and our cottages, a silence settled between us. But now it wasn't filled with awkwardness or his looming aura. It was... comfortable. Easy.

When I turned off the path to my cottage, he shot me a faint smile. "See you in a few hours?"

"Absolutely," I said already planning my wardrobe—business, not casual. "Enjoy your afternoon."

He casually placed his hands in his pockets as he nodded and continued along the path, his smile remaining.

And I felt it again.

That excited flutter in my stomach, a hint of attraction that both excited and terrified me. Clay was not only my boss but also a very attractive man. I'd have to have ice in my veins not to respond to him. Was I imagining a new appreciation, maybe even an appreciative spark, in his eye?

Chapter Seven

Clay

"RIGHT THIS WAY, GENTLEMEN, MS. BRIGGS," Evan Markham said in his deep, professional voice as he led us past the check-in counter and down a quiet hallway. The air was filled with the murmur of guests checking in and the scent of tropical flowers. Once again, I appreciated Evan's discretion in letting us avoid the resort's usual bustle.

"I've arranged a private meeting room for you," he continued, stopping in front of a set of double doors.

Evan pushed the doors open, and I stepped into the room, my gaze sweeping over the space. It was a spacious, light-filled room with floor-to-ceiling windows overlooking the ocean. A large mahogany table dominated the room, surrounded by plush leather chairs. A state-of-the-art video screen was mounted on one wall, flanked by speakers and a podium with a microphone. A pitcher of cucumber-infused water and a plate of delicate pastries sat on a side table.

"This meeting room is quiet and secluded, perfect for whatever you might need." He paused, tilting his head toward me. "Let me know if you need anything at all, Mr. Harmon. I'll make it happen."

"An impressive set-up for a beach resort," I said, nodding my approval. "Though we only require the table for our meeting today."

"Of course," Evan said, his smile unwavering. "You have my number if you need anything." With a final nod, he pulled the doors closed behind him, leaving the three of us alone.

Elise crossed to the side table and poured us each a glass of cucumber water, her movements precise and efficient. She placed the glasses on coasters in front of three chairs, then took her own seat near one end of the table. Pulling her laptop from her bag, she opened it and put on her glasses.

"Thank you, Elise," I said, my gaze lingering on her for a beat too long.

She was the picture of professional composure in her crisp white blouse and navy skirt, her hair neatly twisted into a bun. Such a contrast to the woman who had laughed beside me on the dive boat that morning, her hair a tangle of sun-kissed waves, her skin glowing with warmth and... something else I couldn't quite name. The memory sent a jolt of awareness through me, and I frowned, turning to pull my own laptop out and get to the business at hand.

She glanced up with a quick smile. "Of course. I'm ready when you are."

I pulled out a chair at the head of the table, my gaze sweeping over Bart as he settled into the seat adjacent to me. He was dressed in a crisp white linen shirt and khaki pants, his hair neatly combed. A pleasant contrast from his usual rumpled appearance. He greeted Elise with a respectful nod, his gaze carefully avoiding hers.

I registered this shift with a sense of satisfaction. My

reprimand had clearly had its intended effect. However, I was surprised by the intensity of my reaction to Bart's behavior earlier. Though I made no secret of my zero-tolerance harassment policy, his actions earlier had sparked... I was still struggling to define it. Protectiveness?

I pushed the thought away, determined to maintain my focus. I opened my briefcase and pulled out the competing proposals, spreading them across the table. The familiar numbers and charts were a welcome distraction, their cool logic a comfort against the unfamiliar turmoil of emotion.

"All right," I said, my voice regaining its usual crispness as I took charge of the meeting. "Let's discuss our two potential buyers, then we'll move on to the dinner tonight."

Bart leaned forward, his gaze intent. "Laurent's offer is the most attractive, financially speaking. And something about Celeste Rhodes makes me uneasy."

"Uneasy how?" I asked, intrigued. Bart's instincts for financial matters were usually sharp, even if his personal behavior left something to be desired.

"She's too... eager to please," Bart replied, frowning. "It makes me wonder if she's hiding something."

"Perhaps she's simply a skilled negotiator," I suggested, though I understood Bart's reservations. Celeste's warmth and charisma were disarming, a stark contrast to Laurent's aloof arrogance.

"Maybe," Bart conceded. "But I still think we need to proceed with caution. We can't let her charm us into accepting a lowball offer."

"Agreed," I said, nodding. "Elise, make a note to verify TechWeb's financial statements. I want to be absolutely certain their numbers are solid."

"Already on it," Elise said, her fingers flying across the keyboard of her laptop. "I've also requested a detailed breakdown of their projected revenue over the next five years. I should have that information by this evening."

"Good," I said. Elise's ability to anticipate my needs was one of the things that made her such a valuable asset.

"One more thing," Elise added, her dark blue eyes meeting mine over the rim of her glasses. "Should we anticipate any counteroffers from either party during dinner tonight?"

"It's possible," I replied. "We need to be prepared to respond strategically. Bart, I want you to focus on the financial details. I will handle the negotiation tactics and the overall flow of the conversation. Elise, you jump in if you feel the conversation needs a nudge."

"Understood," Bart said, nodding curtly.

"Yes, sir," Elise added.

I took a sip of the cucumber water, the cool liquid refreshing against my palate. The weight of responsibility for this deal was a constant companion, but I thrived on pressure.

Bart and I continued to dissect each element of the two proposals, exploring various scenarios and mapping out our responses. Elise remained attentive, diligently noting our every word.

"Laurent mentioned his interest in expanding Podium into the European market," Bart said, tapping his finger on a page of his notes. "We might leverage that ambition during the negotiation."

"Yes. We could—" Elise's eyes flashed with surprise as her words stopped.

"Could what?" I prompted.

A delicate flush danced across her face. It made me wonder if her skin would feel warmer there. "I'm sorry," she continued. "I got caught up in thc excitement. It's not my place to interject."

Bart's lips lifted into a hint of a sneer, which pissed me off. "I'd like to hear what you have to say."

"Oh. Well, I was just thinking that you could counter by highlighting the potential challenges of such an expansion. And that Celeste's offer eliminates the need for approvals due to foreign ownership simply because TechWeb is a US company. Laurent might need to be reminded that it's not as simple as replicating Podium's success in a new territory."

"Excellent point," I said, intrigued by her strategic thinking.

She quickly took a gulp of water. "Thank you."

Even Bart looked a little impressed.

Sensing she was still flummoxed, I refrained from pointing out that Laurent's extensive experience with sports and diverse multinational businesses would make for a rather seamless transition. "Don't be afraid to speak up. You're part of the team here."

When she glanced up from her water and met my eyes, I forgot to breathe for a moment as our gazes held. The sight of her in that swimsuit this morning flashed through my brain before I could get a grip on my runaway mind. Wrenching my eyes away, I brought up the next report on my laptop.

The remainder of our meeting passed quickly. We analyzed current market trends, debated legal complexities, and brainstormed ways to maximize Podium's value. Elise ensured every detail was meticulously documented. As the sun began to dip lower in the sky, casting long shadows across the meeting room, I felt a sense of satisfaction. We were prepared.

I leaned back in my chair, flexing my shoulders to ease the tension that had settled there. "Good work," I said, my gaze sweeping over Bart and Elise. "We've covered a lot of ground today."

"Indeed," Bart agreed. "We've got all our bases covered, and I have a feeling we're about to hit a home run with this sale."

"I hope you both managed to take some time to enjoy yourselves this afternoon," I said, the words leaving my mouth before I could stop them. I blinked, surprised at my own question. I rarely inquired about the personal lives of my employees, but the words seemed to hang in the air, demanding an answer.

"I did," Bart replied easily. "Took a walk along the perimeter path. It goes all around the island. Got in some exercise and enjoyed the view. This place is pretty spectacular, even for someone who's more of a city guy."

"I spent some time at the pool. Also, I attended a yoga class yesterday at a studio I came across, Calypso Calm." Elise's gaze met mine briefly, a tentative smile on her lips. "It was... surprisingly relaxing. A great way to let go of stress."

Just the thought of contorting into all those positions nearly made me shudder with distaste. Nate, of all people, had told me he enjoyed yoga. I couldn't fathom any of it. "I find pressure brings out my best work," I replied, my voice clipped and professional. "I have no need to relieve stress."

Elise's smile faltered, and she straightened her belongings absently, her gaze fixed on her closed computer. A sudden awkward silence settled over the room, and what I'd just said came back to me. I'd just reinforced the image of a cold, unfeeling CEO.

The very image Nate had accused me of perpetuating.

"Maybe you should view the people who work for you as, you know, human beings. Not just pieces on a chessboard." Nate's words echoed in my mind, a stark and unwelcome reminder. God, was I really that much of an asshole?

"Right," Elise murmured. She moved her eyes to her notepad, her pen tapping a silent rhythm against the paper.

Bart cleared his throat, shifting uncomfortably in his chair. "Well," he said, forcing a jovial tone. "I'm going to make sure I'm looking my best for tonight. Can't have Laurent thinking we're a bunch of beach bums, can we? Is there anything else?"

I was feeling unaccountably flustered about my words, and it took a moment for his question to sink in. I simply shook my head. "Nothing else. Thank you."

He rose and headed for the door, his escape a palpable relief. As the door clicked shut behind him, I shifted in my seat, the weight of Elise's silence pressing down on me.

"Elise," I began, my voice rougher than usual. "Your insights during our meeting were excellent. Especially that point about the challenges Laurent will face in Europe."

"Thank you." Her voice was soft, but her eyes regained some of their usual glint. "I try to do my best."

"You're excellent at what you do," I said, and a warmth spread through my chest that had nothing to do with the tropical climate outside. "And you're more than welcome to take time for yourself while we're here, yoga included. In fact, I'm glad you found something you enjoy."

My attempt to expand on the compliment felt clunky, the words foreign on my tongue. But, dammit, I wasn't used to expressing regret! And still wasn't sure I should be—I was the boss, after all. Wait, did I even apologize to her?

I hated emotions.

Then a touch of forgiveness flickered in her eyes, and

my chest loosened a little. So maybe my so-called apology wasn't so bad after all.

"Thank you," she repeated, a genuine smile finally gracing her lips. "I appreciate that."

I pushed back my chair and stood, needing to put some distance between us. The air in the room suddenly felt charged, the silence humming with an energy that was new.

"I'm very pleased with how this trip is progressing," I said, my voice softening. "And with your dedication to keeping everything running smoothly." It was the truth. Elise had been invaluable in managing the logistics of the trip and anticipating my every need.

"Thank you, Clay," she replied, her gaze meeting mine directly.

And for some reason, hearing my name on her lips sent a rush of heat straight to my core. To cover my reaction, I closed my laptop and placed it in my briefcase. "Let's each take some time to get ready for dinner," I said, my voice regaining its usual crisp tone. "I'll see you and Bart at Orchid at six forty-five."

I turned and strode out of the meeting room, my footsteps echoing in the quiet hallway. As I walked back to my cottage, I stretched my tight back. The strategy session had been productive, and I was confident we were well-prepared.

But my thoughts kept returning to Elise. To the warmth in her eyes, the sincerity of her smile, her presence next to me during the dive that morning. The memory of those brief moments of connection, of shared laughter and easy conversation, lingered like the floral scent of the bouquet in the living room of my cottage. I shook my head, trying to dispel the unwelcome distraction.

Focus on the deal.

Yet as I entered my cottage and poured myself a glass of Macallan, I couldn't ignore the flutter of anticipation that stirred within me. Tonight was a critical juncture. If last night's reception was the introduction, tonight would be the opening set. But now the night held the promise of something more, something I hadn't anticipated.

Something I wasn't quite ready to name.

Chapter Eight

Clay

I GAZED around the intimate dining area. Like last night, we were once again inside Orchid restaurant, but in a much smaller room this time. Our intimate gathering was warm and inviting. An abundance of fresh orchids were placed around the room, which was dominated by a gorgeous hardwood table and upholstered chairs. The moon cast its silvery light over the dark waters outside. A soft breeze whispered through the room, carrying the scent of the exotic blooms. In addition to Elise and Bart, Celeste and Laurent joined me. The Frenchman hadn't bothered to invite his... mistress? God knew she wasn't his wife.

"What a stunning view," Celeste said, gazing out at the moonlit water. One entire wall was open to the night air.

"Almost as stunning as our lovely dinner companions," Laurent replied smoothly, with an appraising look at Elise that I didn't much care for.

"Cheers to new friends," I said, raising my glass. Four others met mine in the center of the table.

"*Sante*," Laurent replied, clinking his glass against mine. His accent was elegant, but his confidence was off the charts. As we began to eat, I observed Laurent's interactions with the group, noting how he dominated the conversation.

"I own a stable of sports franchises, so adding a sports-betting business is a natural progression. Of course, my teams are under a separate entity, so there would be no conflict of interest."

He cast me a sidelong glance, as if daring me to question him. His demeanor hinted at a ruthlessness that would make dealing with him a challenge. But with Laurent currently having the higher offer, I wouldn't let my personal feelings get in the way of business.

I took a sip of my Bordeaux. Laurent had chosen it, and as expected, it was excellent. "I have no doubt you would usher Podium into a new era seamlessly," I said noncommittally. He met my gaze squarely, neither of us looking away.

Celeste broke the stalemate gracefully. "Too bad France is so far away from Podium headquarters." I turned to see a warm smile on her face. "My father formed TechWeb thirty years ago in Silicon Valley, and I helped bring it into the modern age. Podium would fit beautifully into our business model."

"Your company has a notable history," Bart said, engaging Celeste in conversation. In keeping with his turnaround this afternoon, he acted professionally and showed a rare ability to keep the conversation flowing, which impressed me. He'd proven to be a real asset over dinner, keeping both bidders on point without letting either of them gain the upper hand.

"Thank you, Bart," Celeste replied, her eyes lighting up. "We've worked hard to stay at the forefront of innovation."

"Of course, we have many aspects of the sale to take

into consideration," Bart added with a look at Laurent. "You both present competitive offers."

When there was a lull in the conversation, I cleared my throat. "Though we are all here on business, the night is far too beautiful for nothing but shop talk. Let us enjoy this magnificent setting."

"It is a lovely evening," Elise added as she gazed out at the ocean. A tablet sat on the table next to her, and she'd referenced it several times, looking up items or taking notes. Otherwise, she'd kept her additions to the conversation casual, engaging Laurent and Celeste in non-business topics. In other words, she was doing exactly what I'd asked her to.

Her wardrobe choices for the trip kept me surprised— that swimsuit this morning, then all business this afternoon. Tonight, she wore a shimmering soft-blue evening gown that was sexier than hell without being too provocative. In her evening gown, she was beautiful, a goddess rising from the sea. I grabbed my wineglass and took a healthy sip, displeased at my inability to focus.

Elise turned to the Frenchman. "Laurent, what is your favorite city in France?"

He sent her a smile that made me grip my wineglass. "Any that you might grace with your beautiful presence, *cherie.*"

My assistant navigated this and a couple more of Laurent's flirtations with poise, deflecting him and keeping the conversation on track. I admired her grace under pressure, though my desire to throttle the Frenchman steadily increased.

She'd shown some business acumen I'd never glimpsed during our prep meeting, but diving with her this morning had revealed an entirely new side of her. Despite being unsure at first, she'd jumped into the unknown anyway. Diving with her had brought out a protective side to me, making me want to be near her to help with any difficulties —despite having April with us, who was obviously capable of handling any number of problems or emergencies. Though I still wasn't happy about this new reaction I had to her.

But for myself, being underwater again had been revelatory. Like coming across a favorite book one hadn't read in a long time. Other than my recent pool refresher, I hadn't been in the water in years. I loved every second of it, the feel of the water surrounding me, the bright colors, the inquisitive fish. Being weightless and *free*—the total opposite of my normal life. I couldn't wait to dive again.

But business first.

As dinner continued, the personalities of Laurent and Celeste became even more evident. Laurent's insistence on control made him difficult to navigate, while Celeste's charm and genuine interest in the people around her made her easy to converse with.

"Tell me," Elise said, addressing Laurent and Celeste, "what would you like to do while you're at Calypso Key?"

"Ah, well," Laurent replied with a Gallic shrug. "Tomorrow, I'm flying Irina to Miami for shopping. She is pleasant company for me so I enjoy spoiling her."

I stifled the urge to roll my eyes at the undeclared confirmation that Irina was his mistress. I felt the need to wipe my hands on my pants but refrained.

After a tight-lipped look at Laurent, Celeste let a smile rise as she turned to Elise. "I've always wanted to tour Old Town Key West. I hear it's quite charming."

Elise's eyes widened and she nodded enthusiastically.

"That's a wonderful idea. Why don't I set up a private tour for you?"

"Oh! A tour would be lovely," Celeste said. "That's very thoughtful of you."

It was on the tip of my tongue to compliment Elise's organizing skills, but I held back, worried I might be going overboard. Irritation at myself washed over me like a burn. I'd barely noticed the woman for three years, and now I wanted to be her champion?

She's my assistant! *This is her job, dammit.*

We had a pleasant and productive dinner. I now had a clearer picture of our two top bidders, and the three of us worked well as a team. Elise was charming and professional, and her auburn hair had a beautiful golden tint that made me want to stroke it. Even Bart, who I had never considered particularly engaging, kept things professional and interesting. I found myself reevaluating my opinion of him. He was a good CFO, and maybe this trip would result in an improvement of his attitude.

But despite my best efforts, I couldn't shake my growing attraction toward Elise. Her beauty was undeniable, but it was her poise and the way she made everything run smoothly that impressed me. My life, both professionally and personally, had been much more manageable since her arrival as my assistant. I tried to keep telling myself that she wasn't anything more, but then the strap of her dress would shift, revealing a delicate collarbone.

After a couple glasses of wine, Laurent became more subdued, and I couldn't deny that Podium would be a very appropriate addition to his empire. Celeste continued to charm the table, making a genuine effort to connect with each of us. I remained polite, yet aloof, maintaining my professional demeanor throughout the night.

As the dinner came to a close, my eyes returned yet again to Elise in that gorgeous dress. Wondering what she had on under it, I took a moment to appreciate the elegant line of her neck, unable to block the thought of running a trail of kisses down it. Pursuing anything with her would cross a line I had no intention of breaching, but subtle glances never hurt anyone.

After Laurent and Celeste left, I ordered a bottle of Cabernet for the three of us. We raised our glasses in a toast to our successful trip thus far. We discussed the sale and the two bidders, as well as tomorrow—which would start with another meeting.

"Here's to a successful trip," Bart toasted.

"Cheers," Elise replied, clinking her glass with ours.

After our nightcap, I excused myself, citing the need for some fresh air. I changed into shorts and a T-shirt and went for a barefoot stroll along the beach. It was such a relaxing change to simply enjoy myself as a man instead of a CEO. The waves lapping at my feet brought a sense of peace and tranquility that I hadn't experienced in a long time. A pang of loneliness crept through me, then I pushed it firmly away. My previous relationships had been with women who only wanted me for what they could get from me—what my money and position could provide. I was better off alone.

As I returned to enjoy the night from the pool deck of my cottage, I caught sight of Elise walking along the shore. The silver moonlight illuminated her dress and hinted at the body underneath, making her seem almost ethereal. She carried her shoes in one hand, allowing the water to splash over her feet.

Just as I had done minutes ago.

Her hair cascaded down her back, and the breeze played with the hem of her dress, teasing glimpses of her legs. She moved with an unconscious grace, unaware she was being admired.

"Get it together, man," I muttered to myself, rushing to my feet and marching inside. I closed the door behind me and took a marching step forward. Then I froze. I couldn't stop myself, helpless to keep from turning around to peek through the blinds at Elise as she ambled along the shoreline, the moon casting a radiant light on her face.

Chapter Nine

Elise

I CHEWED my lip as I surveyed my cottage, making sure it was spotless in the morning sun. A recently delivered coffee service filled the room with a rich, enticing scent. I smoothed my pencil skirt, preparing for the strategy meeting with Clay and Bart. The change in venue from Clay's larger cottage to mine was a last-minute change I hadn't expected, but the mystery was solved when Bart walked in a few minutes later.

"I convinced Clay to have the meeting here," Bart said, a smile playing on his lips. "I thought it would be nice to get him off his home turf, so you'd feel more at ease."

"Uh... thank you," I said, though I had no idea what he was talking about. If anything, being around Clay lately did the exact opposite of putting me at ease. And not because he intimidated me. Though I had to admit Bart had been more pleasant to be around after Clay's reprimand. He'd actually impressed me at the dinner last night.

And hopefully a room snafu wouldn't cause any issues

for our meeting. After showering, I'd discovered my bathroom sink faucet was faulty. The water was currently off as maintenance attempted to source the problem from afar.

Clay arrived shortly after, dressed casually in khakis and a button-down shirt that accentuated his athletic build. The lock of hair flopping over his forehead gave him a charming look, and I had a sudden urge to sweep it back in place. I poured us all coffees before we settled into our seats, with Clay across from me on a couch and the coffee table between us.

Bart sat next to me and stretched both arms over his head with a long sigh. "I slept like a log last night. Best sleep I've had in years!"

Clay nodded. "So did I. The bed was extremely comfortable."

A vision of me in it with him popped into my head. An image of sweat and passion, and me stroking that chiseled chest. I quickly took a sip of coffee to cover the heat racing across my face. A quick glance at the open door of my bathroom provided me with a different subject to think about. "Oh, speaking of the resort. The faucet burst in my bathroom this morning. Evan said they'd either fix it or find me another cottage."

Bart snorted. "I thought this was an upscale place."

I shrugged at him. "When I called Evan about it, he was extremely apologetic, and maintenance issues must happen regularly in rooms being used all the time. I'm sure they'll find me something."

"No doubt they will," Clay said absently as he jotted down a note. "Let's get down to business."

He and Bart discussed the two offers on the table, Laurent's and Celeste's, while I typed out notes. While Laurent's proposal was financially more advantageous, working with Celeste seemed like it would be a far more enjoyable experience. Though I knew Clay well enough that he wouldn't let emotions cloud his judgement.

"Ultimately, we won't be working with either of them for long," Clay mentioned, his expression serious.

Bart tapped his index fingers together, eyeing Clay. "True, which makes our decision all the more important. As CFO, my job is to watch the bottom line. And that makes Laurent's offer the only one to consider."

I disagreed but was hesitant to voice my opinion. Yes, financials were important, but so were the employees working for Podium. Clay had mentioned all would receive a generous bonus after the sale, so I remained silent. After all, I was there to help Clay with tasks and logistics, not as a member of the decision team.

Clay was distant during the meeting, hardly noticing me. But Bart made up for it. As the CFO handed out papers, his hand would graze mine. When he poured a glass of water from the pitcher on the center of the table, our arms brushed. His actions were much more subtle than on the boat yesterday, and I couldn't be sure if his touch was intentional or accidental. But it made me uncomfortable. Bart Mayhew was the last man I wanted touching me.

When I scooched away after the water incident, Clay stilled, his icy blue eyes darting between us, only to settle on Bart. Then Clay's phone rang, distracting him.

"What? Now? I'm in a meeting." He paused, listening, then checked his watch. "Fine. Give me five minutes, then have him call me." He lifted his gaze to us as he pocketed his phone and stood. "It's the Tokyo office, calling about GreenDrive. I need to take this."

I frowned and glanced at my tablet. We already had a conference call scheduled later that afternoon with an executive from the electric vehicle tech company, Clay's latest passion. His empire extended to multiple industries—Podium was only a portion of it. I loved both the idea of the acquisition and the thought of being at the vanguard of a field exploding in popularity and importance.

"One of the parties has an emergency and they need to move the call up," Clay explained, sensing my confusion. "I'll keep it as short as possible." And with that, he left the cottage, leaving Bart and me alone. The room now felt emptier, as if some of the life had been sucked out of it.

I wasn't sure if he was coming back or if the meeting was over. But I didn't want to chitchat with Bart, who was swinging back ever closer to being a creep again during our session. I adjusted my glasses and noted the agenda on my laptop screen. "All right, let's continue."

"With what?" Bart asked, leaning back on the couch. "Clay would blow a gasket if we talked business without him."

I drew my brows together. I'd worked as closely with Clay as Bart, and I'd never seen anything like him blowing a gasket. He was too icy, too controlled for that. At least in a business environment...

There I go again, thinking forbidden thoughts.

But the CFO was right. Clay was the one in charge, not either of us. And if the meeting was over, Bart had no reason to remain.

But before I could speak, he cocked his head. "I'm curious. What do you do for fun when you're not working?"

My cheeks warmed up. Maybe a vague answer would send him on his way. "Uh, just the usual. I'm a pretty private person, Bart." Then an idea occurred to me, and I attempted to put him on the spot by asking about his personal life. "So how's your divorce going?" I figured that would make him uncomfortable and put a damper on his curiosity.

To my surprise, his eyes lit up. "Oh, it's going great! Almost finalized!" A smirk spread across his face and a glimmer entered his eye.

Oh, great. Did he think I asked the question to see if he was available?

I wanted to give myself a facepalm.

As if sensing that he had an advantage, Bart slid closer to me on the couch. "In fact, I'm free as a bird now." He leaned in slightly. "Elise, you're a beautiful woman, and you deserve to be treated with a whole lot more respect than our illustrious boss shows. I'm not afraid to have fun once in a while. Would you like a glass of champagne?" He pointed with his chin at the unopened bottle still in its ice bucket that had been waiting when I'd checked in.

"Hell no!" I practically shouted as I vaulted to my feet. "We're here on business, Bart, and you are way out of line." My voice was firm and unwavering as I faced him down. I had been Clay's assistant for three years, and I wasn't about to let some self-absorbed man-child jeopardize my career or my dignity.

"Oh, come on," Bart said, trying to cajole me as he rose to his feet. He glanced around the sunny cottage before settling his eyes on me again. "Loosen up a little. We're in paradise. Might as well take advantage of it." He reached out to touch my arm, but I quickly jerked away.

"Keep your hands off me," I warned, my eyes narrowed.

My heart raced with a mixture of anger and fear. Fear that I'd lose control of the situation, and anger at myself for not throwing Bart out the second Clay left. Feeling cornered and increasingly nervous, I bolted out the front door and onto the covered deck. Bart chased after me, grabbing both of my arms and spinning me around to face him.

"Listen, sweetheart," he snarled quietly, his face inches from mine. "If you say anything to Clay about this, I'll make sure you get fired. I can make life easy for you or very, very difficult. It's your choice. Let's just go back inside and forget all about this little misunderstanding."

I jerked both arms out of his grasp and stared at him, my entire body trembling with rage. "Get. Your. Hands. Off. Me." I spat each word out deliberately, my voice shaking with fury. "Don't you dare touch me again. Do you really think I'm scared of you?" My voice rose with each word.

Bart, taken aback by my sudden outburst, took a step back. I could see the shock in his eyes as he realized I wouldn't be an easy target.

Good, let the son of a bitch understand I'm not going to back down.

"Elise, come on—"

"No! You didn't just cross the line. You goddamn pole-vaulted over it." My voice echoed through the open space of the beach. Heat spread over my face, but I didn't care. I needed to stand up for myself.

"Look, I didn't mean anything by it," he stammered, now backpedaling.

My hands balled into fists at my sides, my nails digging into my palms. "Mean anything by it? You've been touching me all morning, making me feel uncomfortable. Hell, you always do that. And then you chase me out here, threatening my job? That's not a misunderstanding, Bart. It's harassment."

"Fine, I'm sorry," he said, spitting the words out. But his apology rang hollow, a half-hearted attempt to save face.

"No. Sorry doesn't cut it." I fixed him with a fierce gaze,

refusing to let him off the hook. My voice rose, punctuating my words with finality. "You don't treat people like this. You don't make them feel threatened and vulnerable. You don't use power as a weapon to manipulate them."

"Elise—" he tried again, but I wasn't having it.

"Enough!" I bellowed, my voice carrying through the resort like a storm. The last of my patience shattered, leaving me raw and exposed. "Goddammit, Bart, leave me alone!"

Chapter Ten

Clay

I SAT on a lounge chair near my pool, squinting at the glittering surface. As I held the phone to my ear, my free hand gestured in the air to emphasize my point. "I understand the opportunity perfectly well," I said, my voice steely and focused. "The question is whether you and your colleagues do."

The acquisition of an electric vehicle technology company had been ongoing, and I'd left the deal simmering to focus on Podium. Apparently, it had just started boiling. The thrill of exploring uncharted territory, and a new challenge, coursed through my veins. GreenDrive's CEO was now calling about my offer, but he hedged his position with every sentence.

"I've done my research," I continued. "And I've made a generous offer. I have the resources to make GreenDrive a giant in its field. You called me, so I suggest we move negotiations forward. My patience is not limitless."

As engrossed as I was in the conversation, it took a

moment for the raised voices nearby to register in my mind. When they did, I recognized Elise's raised, strained tone and bolted to my feet.

"Mr. Harmon," the Japanese CEO said in his excellent English. "This is a delicate matter, and requires a thorough…"

I quit listening when Elise shouted something else. I couldn't make out exactly what she was saying, but her tone came through loud and clear.

"I have to go. We'll talk later," I said abruptly, hanging up without waiting for a response.

My heart hammered in my chest as I rushed toward Elise's cottage, and I tried to figure out what would cause my calm, unflappable assistant to raise her voice. When I rounded the corner, I found Elise and Bart on her front deck. They faced each other and both Elise's fists were clenched—her teeth were practically bared. She stood tall, asserting herself despite the fear lingering in her eyes.

"Goddammit, Bart, leave me alone!" she screamed, her voice filled with anger and desperation.

That was all I needed to hear. A red curtain descended over my eyes and I started running. Bart's eyes widened as he caught sight of me, and he blanched. I didn't hesitate, racing up the steps and onto the porch.

"What the hell is going on here?" I demanded, though I had a pretty good idea just from what I'd seen and heard so far.

Bart scrambled for words, trying to regain some semblance of control over the situation. "It was a… misunderstanding, Mr. Harmon," he said, his voice cracking. He cleared his throat. "Elise just, um, misconstrued my actions."

My jaw clenched, and I shot Bart a withering glare.

You're back to addressing me formally, huh? I was already itching to throw a punch. This wasn't just some petty squabble or misunderstanding. Raw emotion was written all over Elise's face.

"Like hell I did, you asshole," Elise spat, her voice tight and shaking. Then she jerked her head to stare wide-eyed at me, as if she just realized she'd sworn in front of her boss.

But I didn't get a chance to reassure her that I thought a few cuss words were entirely appropriate.

When I saw the red handprint on Elise's arm, the rest of the world disappeared. My pulse roared in my ears. The very thought of Bart laying hands on her sent a surge of rage through me. I stormed up to him, pointing at the mark on her arm.

"Did you do this?" I demanded, my voice low and dangerous.

Bart opened and closed his mouth like a fish out of water, but no words came out. It was all the confirmation I needed.

"You're fired," I snarled.

Elise stared at me with her mouth hinged open, but that only fueled my resolve further.

Bart blinked a few times before his face contorted into a sneer. "I'm the CFO! You need me for the Podium sale. You can't fire me."

"Oh, yes, I can. I am."

"I have rights! There's a process for this."

My right hand curled into a fist. "So sue me. In fact, I dare you to." I stepped forward until we were inches apart, towering over him. "Do you really think there is any portion of my business that I don't know backward and forward? You are nothing more than a regulatory require-ment. I can replace you at will. You have half an hour to make flight arrangements and get out of here. On your own dime."

Bart staggered back, shocked. "How am I supposed to do that?"

I arched a brow, still pissed enough to wrestle a lion. "That is not even remotely my concern. Or Elise's. Leave here now or I'm calling security. Assuming I don't beat the living shit out of you right now."

Bart's face went white, and his eyes darted between Elise and me. "All right. I'm leaving."

"Thirty minutes, Bart," I said with frozen rage.

Without another word, he slinked away from us, scurrying across the sand toward his cottage.

Elise stared at me like I was a stranger, shocked at the intensity of my anger. I was surprised by it myself. It wasn't like me to get so worked up, but that handprint on Elise's arm made me want to pummel Bart into the ground.

"Are you all right?" I asked, softening my voice.

At my words, relief washed over her face. "I'm fine, thanks. And thank you."

Blood still sang through my body. I felt like a goddamn caveman, ready to knock someone over the head with my club. Yet her simple gratitude made me tongue-tied and flustered. "Is there anything... I can do to help?" I asked, stumbling over my words.

Elise hesitated for a moment, her eyes searching mine. Then she offered a small smile and shook her head. "No, this trip just got a whole lot easier. I can't believe you fired him!"

I shrugged, still unsure why she brought out this protective side of me. "We're better off without him."

"Podium doesn't need Bart Mayhew, for sure."

Except I hadn't meant the company. I'd meant her and

me. My reaction had been much more than defending an employee against harassment.

I'd been defending *her*.

Because I had just discovered that part of my fury about him touching her was because I wanted to do that myself. But utterly, completely opposite of how he'd done it. When Elise screamed my name, it would be for very different reasons.

———

LATER THAT AFTERNOON, I skirted Dorado and the resort pool on my way to the lobby to speak with Evan. As I passed the bar, I spotted Elise sitting alone and staring into her beer with a glum expression. Concern slowed my steps.

Earlier, after insisting she was all right, she'd gone back inside her cottage. I'd returned to my own and called my legal team to make sure Bart couldn't get a leg up on me, though I wasn't overly worried. He wasn't the type to go up against the alpha wolf. My lawyers agreed but assured me they would send him a nice letter stating the facts. Then I'd called the GreenDrive CEO back and had a more productive conversation. After the gala, we would proceed with negotiations.

I hadn't seen Elise until now, and I couldn't help wondering if leaving her alone had been wise. But what was I supposed to do when she'd told me she was okay? I wasn't her keeper. I was still trying to decipher my reaction to this morning's events—that possessive, righteous anger that had taken hold of me. A milder version of which was making my blood hum right now.

I didn't even stop to think, and my feet detoured from

my path as I headed toward the bar. I had to see her. Approaching, I slid into the seat next to her.

"Hey," I said quietly, trying to gauge her mood. "How are things this afternoon?"

She sighed, her fingers tracing the condensation on the glass. "So-so. After the high of you getting Bart out of our hair, it turns out the resort can't fix my room without some major parts. They're working on finding me another cottage."

"That doesn't sound good," I muttered.

Before I could say anything else, Evan strode up, obviously having spotted us. "Mr. Harmon, I'm glad I found you. Good afternoon, Elise."

"Hello, Evan," she replied, attempting a smile that didn't quite reach her eyes.

"Is Bart gone?" I asked him, wanting to make sure that issue was settled.

"Yes. I personally saw him off the premises and confirmed he had a plane ticket to New York."

"Good. Thank you for your assistance." I nodded, pleased to have the issue settled. "Now, about Elise's new cottage. Is it ready?"

Evan swallowed and shook his head. "I'm sorry. That's why I came to find you two. The resort is at maximum occupancy right now, and we're struggling to find an alternative room for Elise. We're looking into nearby resorts."

My gaze narrowed at Evan, my voice firm. "That is unacceptable. What about Bart's cottage? Surely that's available now."

"Unfortunately, another guest already occupied it," Evan replied. "I'm very sorry. We're working right now with a nearby resort to accommodate Elise. We'll confirm the new room is of the highest quality, I assure you."

My teeth ground as frustration rose inside me. My next words tumbled out of my mouth. "Absolutely not. We have far too much to do before the gala. Elise, you can stay in my cottage." I blinked in surprise at my own offer. I wasn't one to share my living quarters with anyone. But I meant it. I couldn't have her staying somewhere else when so much was on the line.

Elise's hand froze, the glass halfway to her mouth. Her eyes grew round. "What?"

It was too late to backpedal now, and I didn't second guess my decisions. "You heard me. If Evan can't find you another room here, then you stay with me."

She slowly set her glass back on the bar top, leaving her hands wrapped around it. "That's very generous of you, but I'm fine staying at a nearby resort. I can rent a car."

I scowled, turning to face her. "We are days from cementing the biggest business deal of my career. And yours. I need you nearby, and you don't have to worry about us... mingling. There are two bedrooms in my cottage."

Evan nodded and gave her a hopeful smile. "And two private baths as well. You won't need to share any private quarters."

Her conflict was evident in the deep line between her brows. I lifted my eyes to Evan, pinning him with my stare. "You are positive you can't accommodate her anywhere else here on Calypso Key?"

His throat bobbed as he swallowed. "Well, we have a cottage in our private section of the island. It's reserved for Markham family, but it's been out of service for a very long time and not up to our level of guest rooms. If you'd like, I could get housekeeping up there to start cleaning immediately."

Elise bolted upright. "No. That's silly. I'm not crashing

your personal home, Evan. Though I appreciate the gesture."

Honestly, so did I. As frustrated as I was about the situation, I understood how things went sideways sometimes in business. And I'd seen enough glimpses of the stately manor in the northeast section of the island to understand the area was strictly a private residence.

Elise's eyes bounced between us, then she gave me a small nod. "All right. I'll stay in your spare bedroom. Thank you for the offer."

"Then it's settled," I said. "Let's get you moved immediately."

Evan chimed in, his demeanor brightening. "I'll make sure the staff knows about the change in accommodations, and someone will be by to transfer your luggage. If there's anything else you need, let me know. Again, I'm terribly sorry for the inconvenience. I'll make sure you are suitably compensated."

"Thank you, Evan," Elise said. When she moved her gaze to me, the warmth in her eyes sent a jolt through me. "And thank you again. You didn't have to do this, but I appreciate it."

"Of course," I responded as we rose to our feet, getting that flustered feeling again as our eyes locked. That ridiculous urge to be her champion. Her defender.

As Elise disappeared into her cottage to pack her belongings, I rushed back to mine. A strange thrill coursed through me as I unlocked the door. My brother and I both had neat freak tendencies, so I wasn't worried the place would be too out of line. But I needed to give the cottage a once-over just to make sure.

I went to work tidying up, straightening already neatly stacked papers and rearranging the throw pillows on the couch. Then I decided the housekeeper knew where they belonged better than I did and put them back. Hissing, I told myself my pounding heart was due to exertion, not nerves.

Never mind that I worked out nearly every day.

Moving down the hall, I stopped at the other bedroom and pushed open the door. After taking in the neatly made king-sized bed and well-arranged décor, I grabbed an extra set of towels from the linen closet and placed them on the bed.

"God, what is wrong with me?" I snapped at myself, pacing back and forth in the hallway. "I've dated movie stars, heiresses. Why am I nervous about sharing a cottage with my assistant?"

I paused, leaning against the wall. Then I raked a hand through my hair.

I was nervous because something had happened in the last couple days.

Elise wasn't just my assistant anymore. Until this trip, I'd never really seen her. But since my jet landed in Key West, that had changed. She was smart, capable, and... heart-stoppingly beautiful.

Just as I straightened up, I heard a knock at the door. Ignoring the way my stomach suddenly filled with tumbling rocks, I strode down the hall. I swung the door open to find Elise standing there with a slightly red face. A bellhop stood behind her with her suitcase.

"Hi," she said, shifting from one foot to the other. "You're sure I'm not intruding?"

"Of course not," I said firmly and hopefully reassuringly as I stepped aside to let them in. I directed the bellhop to the bedroom she would be using. "I won't have you staying at another resort, Elise. This is simply the easiest solution."

As a hesitant smile creased her face and I caught a subtle yet exotic floral scent wafting off her hair, I recognized my statement for the lie it was. But this woman was strictly off-limits, especially given what had just happened between her and Bart.

Then again, we'd worked side by side for over three years. Why should sharing the same cottage change anything?

Chapter Eleven

Elise

AS I EXAMINED my new bedroom, a wave of uncertainty washed over me. Soft white linens and plush blue throw pillows adorned the bed, inviting me to sink into their comfort. A modern, ergonomic chair and practical, yet beachy desk against the wall were waiting for me and my laptop. In other words, the room was similar to the one I'd just vacated. Except it was in *Clay Harmon's* cottage. I didn't know whether to be thrilled or terrified, so I figured my current panicked jumble of both was appropriate.

The bedroom featured sliding doors that opened to the private pool area I'd passed on my way in. As promised, Clay's bedroom was on the other side of the joint living area, ensuring plenty of privacy for me.

Clay's bedroom.

My boss's bedroom.

I tried to shake off the sense of being an intruder. But as I settled my belongings inside the stunning wooden dresser, I reminded myself that things could be worse. What if Clay hadn't interceded with Bart when he did? I had no doubt I could have chased the perv off, but I would have had to put up with him for the remainder of the trip. I'd been utterly shocked when Clay fired him. I'd expected a stern talking-to, but part of me had glowed over how quickly Clay had come to my defense. How he never doubted my side of the story.

I strolled across the room to investigate the bathroom. It was larger and more luxurious than my old one, with a large marble tub and walk-in shower. Finally giving into my need to anchor myself, I pulled out my laptop and sat at the desk. Soon I was immersed in spreadsheets and schedules, and my unease slipped away.

The sound of splashing water drew my attention to the pool outside. I got a shock when I glanced at my watch—two hours had passed. I stood and stretched, my tight muscles confirming I'd sat for too long. An idle thought of booking another yoga class flitted through my mind when sunlight glinting off the pool drew my eye. Curiosity got the better of me, and I slowly pulled apart the blinds on the slider, catching a glimpse of Clay as he swam laps in the private pool. My eyes traced the contours of his toned muscles and quickly tanning skin, illuminated by the golden rays of the setting sun. He moved with such easy power, commanding the water around him like a force of nature.

After he emerged from the pool, droplets of water cascading down his body, he took a quick phone call on the deck. A patter of drops fell from his loose board shorts. The entire trip, he'd never worn anything overly suggestive or been forward with me in any way. Yet every time our eyes met, our gazes held like a tractor beam. I couldn't be imagining it! As he spoke into his phone, his demeanor exuded authority and confidence. His wealth or power weren't what made him like the king of the world.

It was simply who he was.

As I stood there, still peering through the blinds, it hit me all at once. I took a firm step back. Despite our proximity, he remained my boss, and I needed to remember that. Clay Harmon was one of the most eligible men on the planet, and I was his *assistant*. I lived in the real world, not some children's fable.

"Get it together, Elise," I whispered to myself, stepping away from the slider and drawing a long breath. "You're here for work, not romance." And I knew better than anyone that nothing but grief came from believing in fairy tales. My gaze fell on the tattered resin angel I'd placed on the dresser earlier and held fast.

The memory crashed into my head like a train. I was ten years old and had spied a beautiful crystal cat sculpture in a boutique window display while walking with my father on a bitterly cold December afternoon. Glinting in the sun, the sizeable figure was nearly round as the feline sat with its tail curled around its paws. Even that young, I'd instantly known it was much too expensive for our struggling family. Dad noticed my fixation on the cat.

"Look at that," he said with a wink. "Christmas is coming up, isn't it? Wouldn't that make an amazing gift?"

I was past the Santa stage at that point, so I just shook my head. "No, it's all right. It looks like it costs a lot."

He reared back, his brown hair ruffling in the cold breeze. "Nothing's too expensive for my princess! I've got a bonus coming later this week. You just wait until Christmas morning."

And so I had, my anticipation and naive belief growing every day. Especially once a heavy square box appeared in shiny wrapping paper under our tree. On the big morning, I'd raced to our living room with Mom and Dad,

Mom laughed at my enthusiasm. "He wouldn't tell me what was in it. I'm as excited as you are!"

I ripped off the paper hiding my wonderful cat, then stared at the box within. Confusion filled me when I hefted the box up to my face and beheld the blue speckled object inside. "Is this a... bowling ball?" I'd never seen one in person, but I recognized it.

Dad's face was now the color of a ripe tomato. "Well, that ol' bonus didn't come through like I thought. Sorry, princess."

I refused to allow the tears that wanted to fill my eyes. Mom just stared at him. "What is she supposed to do with a bowling ball, Terry?"

His face became animated. "I thought you and I could learn to play together, Elise! I joined a bowling league. Our games are on Sundays at seven in the evening, so it's perfect."

Mom's face turned to stone. "I do not want my daughter hanging around with a bunch of drunks on Sunday lamenting the end of the weeken—"

"No," I interrupted, understanding exactly what was going on. And making a decision. "I want to learn to play." I took no small satisfaction from the shocked look on Dad's face at hearing my news. I turned to my mother. "Thank you. I won't let it interfere with school. This ball is my Christmas present, so I mean to enjoy it."

And I had. I'd gone to the bowling alley week after week, struggling and learning. Stuffing tissue around my fingers so they fit in the holes better. All while learning to never get my hopes up. Never to believe in empty promises. And several years later, I won the league championship.

Dad's gift hadn't been malicious—that was the saddest part. He was right there teaching his unlikely acolyte. Though I never forgot that wide-eyed surprise when I'd agreed to his plan. He'd hugged me tight when I won, telling me how proud he was.

But it was my mother who appeared at my bedside the next night and presented me with the resin angel. Six inches long, it was simple, yet elegant. Something she'd obviously paid for from her meager earnings as a seamstress.

She brushed back the hair from my forehead. "Never forget you're an angel. Your father sometimes acts before he thinks, but he loves you. I love you too."

And now every time I looked at that angel, it was a reminder that sometimes all the love in the world wasn't enough. That you had to create your own story.

Because sometimes fairy tales weren't even for children.

With a bittersweet smile, I approached the dresser and pressed my lips to the angel. I gently placed it back on the wooden top. As I glanced around the room again, profound satisfaction filled me. Despite the maintenance problem, I was in this room and on this trip because I was damn good at my job. I was appreciated and paid well for that.

And if I was getting a little thumpy-hearted for my boss? Well, Clay Harmon wasn't exactly Prince Charming, was he? I grinned broadly as I picked up a book and settled on the couch to read. Not being Cinderella, I wasn't about to do drudge work the whole time I was in paradise.

LATER, Clay knocked on my bedroom door and escorted me to dinner. With Bart gone, it was just us. As we walked toward Orchid, his charcoal-gray designer suit only added to his already striking appearance. Once again, he'd gone for a more tropical vibe with a sunny yellow tie. I wore a swishy lavender dress. It was pretty and whimsical, yet professional enough for a business setting.

The hostess seated us at a secluded outdoor table for two overlooking the ocean, where the soft glow of candlelight and the delicate scent of potted orchids surrounded us. The gentle ocean breeze rustled the hair around my face. This setting was much more intimate than the community dinners we'd had so far, and a ripple ran through my belly. I tried to tamp it back down.

Clay studied the wine list for a moment before ordering a bottle of something red and French. After the server poured some for each of us, he raised his glass and proposed a toast, the corner of his mouth twitching up. "To keeping life unpredictable."

Our conversation began with a discussion of changes necessitated by Bart's absence. Clay's demeanor became cooler and more professional, reinforcing that he could handle any financial situations that might arise. Not that I had any doubt. I offered to help with any extra work he might need and let him know the altercation with Bart wouldn't affect my work.

A gleam entered his eye as he replied, "Yes, I'm becoming quite acquainted with your abilities. And your determination."

My cheeks flushed at his words, and I smiled while I tried to determine if he was flirting with me.

As we enjoyed our entrees, Clay leaned in and told me he'd like me to accompany him in the morning to a meeting with both bidders and ensure they had everything they needed. Gratification surged through me at the trust he was placing in me, and made me want to rise to the challenge even more.

Throughout the evening, I found myself letting my guard down, becoming more relaxed around him. That unspoken connection between us grew stronger. Clay opened up about the pressure he'd been under. His eyes drifted around the romantic restaurant, then over the ocean before us. "Being here on semi-vacation makes me realize I do nearly nothing but work. My only other regular activity is exercise."

I listened intently, still surprised at this other side of him. My mind wandered back to the image of him swimming in the pool earlier. My eyes dropped to his mouth. What would it be like to kiss him? To dance my fingers over that sculpted chest?

To be taken by him...

Bart manhandling me had filled me with revulsion and fury, but the idea of Clay holding my wrists immobile sent a flush of arousal through me. I quickly shook off the thought, trying to focus on our conversation.

"Everyone needs a break sometimes," I said softly, swirling my wine. "Maybe you just needed someone to remind you of that."

A long moment passed between us. Neither of us said anything, and I was somewhat taken aback at my bold words. I would never have dared say something like that to him in New York. Yet here it had seemed the most natural thing in the world. Inhaling some courage, I decided to share my own aspirations. After all, if I couldn't be honest with him now, when could I? "I've always hoped for a more substantial role within one of your companies, and I recently earned my MBA. I'd like to apply the next time an appropriate job opens up."

Clay raised an eyebrow, and his stare turned evaluative. "I had no idea, but I certainly don't want to hold you back. Though that will leave me without the best assistant I've ever had."

"Maybe you can find someone almost as good," I teased. As I flipped a lock of hair over my shoulder, his eyes followed the movement, lingering on my neck before rising to my face again.

"Almost as good, huh?" He laughed softly, his eyes glinting in a way that made me press my legs together. "I suppose I might have to settle for that."

Our gazes locked again, something of a precipice between us. This wasn't just about work anymore, and I couldn't deny the attraction that had been building steadily since our arrival. Even his voice was different—rich and deep, without the hard edge. Our conversation continued to flow, as if we'd been friends for years rather than manager and assistant. A tingle flickered down my spine at the way Clay's fingers brushed mine when he passed the breadbasket, or how his foot errantly touched mine once under the table.

"You want to go diving again?" he asked.

"I'd love to, but I'm not sure we've got time before the gala."

He took a sip of the rich wine. "I'm the boss. I make the schedule."

And just like that, another image flooded my senses. Of him naked above me, pinning me in place. I opened my mouth to take a deep breath, and he stared at my lips.

"Maybe tomorrow afternoon when we've finished the meetings." His voice was like velvet, and his strong hand covered mine briefly before he withdrew it. The warmth of his touch lingered on my skin.

"I'd love that," I replied, trying to keep my voice steady. My pulse raced at the thought of spending more time with him outside of business.

Just then, lightning lit up the distant horizon, and the low rumble of thunder followed. The sudden shift in the atmosphere yanked me back to reality.

I'm flirting with Clay Harmon! Have I lost my mind?

With panic rising in my chest, I realized that we should be wrapping up our dinner. I quickly switched gears. "So, we'll meet with Laurent first thing tomorrow morning, then Celeste?" I made sure my voice contained no hint of my inner turmoil.

"Yes," he said quietly. He leaned casually with one elbow on the table, rubbing a finger over the rim of his wineglass. Even though we were back to discussing business, he was nearly irresistible. I didn't know whether I was relieved or disappointed when his expression finally changed, becoming businesslike once again. "We'll secure their final offers then. Nate and Camille arrive tomorrow afternoon, so we can discuss the bids over dinner at our place."

My abdomen lurched at *our place*. How easily he'd said that.

We exited the restaurant and made our way back to the cottage, the night air caressing my skin as we walked side by side. Once inside, I hesitated in the living room, not quite ready to say good night. Our eyes met, that magnetic pull between us snapping into place. Pulsing. As if we were two opposing forces, an unseen power drawing us together.

"Thank you for tonight and for letting me stay here," I murmured, attempting to maintain some semblance of professionalism.

"Thank you for joining me," he replied softly, his voice

sending a quiver tickling down my spine. "Good night, Elise."

"Night."

I turned and made my way to my bedroom, my heart pounding in my chest. I shut the door and leaned back against it, my chest heaving and electricity humming through my body. As I settled into bed, our evening together replayed in my mind. The easy conversation, the growing chemistry crackling between us.

I'm not imagining his interest in me, am I?

Except maybe the bigger question was: if I wasn't imagining it, could I risk seeing where his interest would lead? As much as I might be thinking about this new attraction, I couldn't afford to let it burn me.

Chapter Twelve

Clay

AS THE BIRDS outside sang their usual morning chorus, I cast a glance around the sizeable room. The living room of the two-bedroom cottage was filled with the scent of the fresh flowers Evan had delivered while Elise and I prepared for our meeting with Laurent. Looking in the mirror, I straightened my Brioni suit, anticipation racing through my veins. Dispensing with the tropical-colored ties, I'd chosen power red this morning.

"Are you expecting Laurent to present the stronger final offer?" Elise asked from the couch, a laptop open on her thighs and glasses perched on her nose. She was also dressed for business in a crisp suit with her hair neatly tucked into a bun.

I pushed away the momentary desire to unfurl it and run my fingers through the silky strands. After that emotionally charged dinner, I'd expected to be up half the night, trying to avoid going to her room. But instead, I'd dropped off to sleep immediately.

Thank God for small mercies.

"I'd be surprised if he didn't," I replied. "He likes to think he's the top dog in any negotiation."

The doorbell rang, signaling Laurent's arrival. Elise opened the door, and the Frenchman swept in. He was alone, which surprised me. I had expected a full business entourage, his effort to look more impressive. My opinion of him ticked up a little. He wore an expensive black pinstriped suit, and his eyes held an arrogant gleam as he glanced around the cottage.

"Laurent, welcome," I greeted him, extending my hand.

"*Bonjour*," Laurent said, shaking my hand firmly.

"How was your day yesterday?" Elise chimed in, trying to maintain pleasantries as she poured him a cup of coffee. "Did you enjoy your time in Miami?"

"It cost me a fortune," he said, his eyes roaming up and down her as he accepted the coffee. I tried not to stiffen. "Irina insisted on spending the entire day shopping." Then he turned to look me in the eye. "Enough about that. Why is your assistant here?"

"Elise is essential to the proceedings," I said evenly. "She will keep an official record of everything."

Elise picked up her laptop and balanced it on her lap, while Laurent took a stroll around the area, inhaling the fragrance of the expansive bouquet on the dining room table. Then he frowned as he returned to me in the seating area. "Interesting choice, hosting a multibillion-dollar sale and gala in this backwater location."

I smiled coolly, unperturbed by his condescending tone. "Sometimes it's enjoyable to unplug from the chaos of the city."

He arched a brow as he sat across from me. "Then you

are living in the wrong city. I assure you, Paris would change your outlook."

As we turned to business, I maintained my impartiality despite my dislike for Laurent. After he passed over a manila envelope with a single piece of paper inside, I showed no reaction to the very high number he offered for Podium. Laurent was clearly aware of its value, but his superior manner grated on my nerves.

"Your company may be valuable, but without a CFO, I'd say my offer is more than generous," he said. "Perhaps too generous. Obviously there are cracks in your organization I wasn't apprised of."

I hid my irritation that he already knew about Bart, though I wasn't surprised he had an extensive network. "Let me assure you that Bart's departure will have no repercussions. I am highly skilled in operating all areas of my companies and can ensure a smooth financial transition," I reassured him, hoping to put an end to his insinuations. I refused to discuss specifics of what had happened. "And I imagine Podium's new owner will want to install their own finance team, so the loss of a single member of my staff is a non-issue as far as I'm concerned."

As the meeting continued, I focused on keeping up my cool, detached manner, determined to do what was best for Podium and everyone involved. Elise understood her role and seamlessly faded into the background, except when I needed a figure or document. She anticipated my needs perfectly.

"You present a very strong offer," I said as I stood.

Laurent rose to his feet and shook my hand. "I have made it a practice to get what I want. And I want Podium. Though I must ask, isn't it rather childish to celebrate the winner at the stroke of midnight?"

I shrugged, both hands in my pockets. "On the contrary. It has a poetic elegance I rather like. However, we will announce the new owner earlier that day. The gala is simply a celebration."

After the royal pain in the ass left, Elise busied herself straightening up and removing all traces of Laurent, while I looked over last-minute financials. At 10:00 a.m., the doorbell chimed again, right on time.

"Good morning, Celeste," I greeted her after Elise opened the door to our second potential buyer. I gestured toward the couch across from me. Celeste's hair was styled in an elegant twist and her warm smile was the opposite of Laurent's.

"Thank you for meeting with me," she said as she sat, clothed in a designer skirt suit. Elise set a cup of coffee and a croissant before her. "And thank you, Elise, for arranging the lovely Key West tour yesterday. I had a wonderful time, though my assistant was rather put out that your itinerary was so much better than the one she arranged for me." She turned to me. "You're really fortunate to have such a great assistant, Clay. Mine are a revolving door."

I glanced at Elise, who shot me a subtle, yet extremely challenging stare after thanking Celeste. It went straight to my core, a deep throbbing that made me shift my position. I held her gaze for a moment, trying to school my reaction.

Why does she have to be my assistant?

"Yes, Elise has proven herself over and over." I felt like I should say more, but the satisfaction flitting across her face at least put me at ease. And this was hardly the time or place to wax poetic about her.

Celeste wasted no time in presenting TechWeb's offer to me. "We believe in maintaining the family-oriented approach and commitment to tradition that has made

Podium so successful," she explained, her tone genuine and passionate.

"Thank you for the offer and your interest," I replied, careful to remain neutral after I gave the offer a quick once over. "You present a persuasive case, and I'll give it serious consideration." I would never let on which company I favored, although hearing her enthusiasm was refreshing after dealing with Laurent. Unfortunately, her offer wasn't as compelling financially.

"I would like to clarify something, though," she said, concern in her eyes. "I heard a rumor that Bart left the resort rather abruptly."

"There was a last-minute staffing reassignment," I said, keeping my face completely neutral. "Bart is no longer in that role, but I have an extensive number of staff who are very familiar with the sale. I don't anticipate any impact."

"Understood." Celeste nodded, accepting my explanation without further prying and we moved on to the specifics of her offer.

At the end of the meeting, Elise again offered to arrange any trips or activities Celeste might need, but she declined. "I think I'll just enjoy some beach and pool time before the big gala." She turned to me with a smile. "Thank you again for arranging this trip. What a wonderful way to issue Podium into its new phase, just as the year changes over too! Very exciting."

As we wrapped up our meeting, I appreciated Celeste's professionalism and candor, both a stark contrast to Laurent. But ultimately, our decision would come down to what was best for Podium and its future. And us.

"Thank you once again for your time, Celeste," I said as I saw her out. "We'll see you soon."

"Looking forward to it," she replied with a smile before departing.

As I closed the door, the decision weighed heavy on me. It wouldn't be an easy one, but I didn't have to make it alone. "Nate texted me earlier that he and Camille were about to board the jet. They're on schedule to join us for dinner."

Elise nodded. "I have it arranged with room service. They'll deliver the meal here to the cottage at seven p.m. As for today, your next meeting is at noon and another at two. Then you get a little time to relax before dinner." She twitched her lips with the last sentence.

I shrugged, smiling in return. "No rest for the wicked. I need to call Nate and update him on the offers. At least this time gap gives you some downtime. Enjoy your afternoon, and I'll see you at dinner."

AT SEVEN O'CLOCK, Nate and Camille walked into the cottage, arm in arm and wearing matching smiles. Two years younger than me but several inches taller, Nate and I shared dark-brown hair and blue eyes. He moved with the graceful, athletic form of a former pro hockey player, draping one arm over Camille's athletic shoulders. Their happiness was infectious, and I couldn't help but smile as my brother pulled me in for a quick hug.

"Did you miss me?" he asked, clapping me on the back.

"It hasn't been that long," I replied and turned to greet Camille with an embrace. She had grown up next door to us in Westport, Connecticut, and looked ready for some sun with her hair coiled into a casual bun on top of her head.

Her dark-blonde strands still showed lighter highlights from a summer spent outdoors.

When I informed Nate that Elise was joining us for dinner, he gave me a long, curious look that I ignored. I wasn't sure what exactly was happening between us, but I didn't want her feeling excluded. She swept into the room wearing blue linen pants and a sleeveless blouse, the perfect blend of business and casual. Her hair was down and curling around her shoulders as she took charge of seating us and dealing with the room service delivery. I had to grip my wineglass to resist the urge to stroke a finger down the velvety skin of her arm.

Camille kept the conversation light when I wanted to dig too deep into our prospective bidders, updating us on her and Nate's hockey foundation. It reminded me of his previous observation that I was a joyless workaholic—at least now I recognized my tendencies. Elise and Camille hit it off right away, discussing some hit television show I'd never heard of. My gaze wandered Elise's way several times over the meal, especially when a light, sweet scent drifted my way from her. Because I didn't think it was perfume. I was pretty sure it was *her*.

Eventually, the conversation between Nate and me circled back to business. We discussed the offers from both Laurent and Celeste, weighing the pros and cons of keeping Podium a family-run business or taking Laurent's more lucrative offer.

As the meal wore down, Nate sounded as torn as I was about which offer to take. "I met with both of them this afternoon after we arrived," he noted, setting his napkin on his empty plate. "Laurent's offer is tempting, but Celeste's approach feels more, I don't know... authentic, I guess."

"I agree," I said, still undecided myself. "We need to hash this out some more."

"It's a huge decision for you two," Camille said, then turned to Elise with a wink. "Why don't you and I take a dip in the pool while the boys talk shop?"

Elise hesitated for a moment before agreeing, and the two women left us to change into their swimsuits.

"Want a beer?" I asked, already heading for the minibar fridge. Nate nodded, and we settled down across from each other on couches.

"All right," Nate said as I handed him the bottle. "Enough about Podium for the moment. What's going on between you and Elise?"

My stomach lurched. "Nothing. We're just sharing a cottage because of a mix-up with her room. We have separate bedrooms." I tried to sound casual as I took a sip of my beer, hoping Nate would drop it.

"Come on, Clay. You and Elise had a weird current running between you during dinner. That is definitely new." He gave me a long, knowing look.

I sighed. Maybe it would help to talk about it. Exorcize the demon. "Okay, fine. Maybe I'm starting to see her differently. But she works for me. Nothing's going to happen between us."

Nate draped an arm across the back of the couch. "It's okay to let go once in a while."

I gaped at him, incredulous. "With my *assistant?*"

He cocked his head, reading my thoughts. "I'm not saying it'll be easy, but I caught her sneaking some glances at you tonight."

I stared at him, putting an edge of steel in my eyes. "I fired Bart yesterday. For harassing Elise."

His eyes went round. "Are you shitting me?"

"Most definitely not shitting you."

"He always was an asshole." Nate shrugged, his expression unapologetic. "I see your problem now, but life isn't always neat and tidy. You're sure as hell not Bart Mayhew, and I'm sure Elise realizes that. If you want something badly enough, you'll figure it out. Same with her."

I just stared at him. At this new, mature Nate. "It's not that easy. In fact, it's a veritable minefield."

"So was the situation between me and Camille. When was the last time you let go with a woman?"

I scowled. "I never let go with women. Every woman I've ever been with has only wanted what I could provide."

He just shot me a deadpan look. "Then maybe you need to start seeing different women, huh? Elise is hardly your usual type. This seems like the perfect setup to me."

No. It was a non-issue. "I'm not sleeping with my assistant."

"Whatever, man. It's your call. All I'm saying is maybe you need to take a chance."

I huffed out a long sigh. "I don't take chances. I have no idea what will happen between us. If anything."

"Well, Calypso Key seems to be a place where romance happens no matter what you intend." He tipped his bottle up to finish his beer. "Anyway, I should get going. I'm just going to point out that Camille and I also arrived at this resort as friends and left as a couple. So don't act like it's impossible."

I was going to answer that it was impossible, but the words wouldn't come out. "We'll see, I guess. Thanks for the talk." I managed a weak smile, still processing what he'd said.

"Anytime, brother."

He clapped me on the shoulder before heading out the

door. I heard voices as he and Camille said good night to Elise. Only then did it occur to me that Nate and I had never discussed the Podium sale despite the women giving us privacy. Because I couldn't get Elise off my mind. And now I needed to decide what came next.

Chapter Thirteen

Elise

AFTER AGREEING to the after-dinner swim with Camille, I headed toward my room. I picked up the damp mound of black fabric from my bathroom floor and grimaced at the cold, clammy feel in my hand. My sporty one-piece swimsuit was still soaked from my beach frolicking earlier in the afternoon. I hadn't thought twice before leaving it wadded on the floor, but now I regretted that big time.

Leaving it draped over a towel rack, I padded out of the room and opened a dresser drawer. I glanced at the dark-red bikini neatly folded inside, its silky fabric beckoning me. It was a little daring, but it was dry. I hesitated, then reminded myself that I'd only be with Camille. Why would she be bothered by what I wore?

After changing, I stepped onto the pool deck, where Camille was dipping a toe in the water. She wore a sunny yellow bikini that accentuated her toned physique.

"Oh, good, you're wearing a two-piece also." I tried to

sound casual despite the flush heating my face. "The swim-suit I've been using needs to dry out."

Camille just laughed, her eyes twinkling. "Honey, please. You look fantastic! And who cares? I'm all about comfort and practicality, especially on vacation."

She gestured toward the shimmering turquoise water. "Let's go!" And with that, she dove gracefully into the deep end of the pool.

Yeah, Clay's private pool had a deep end.

I descended the steps, the cool water a welcome relief against my skin. Camille was right—it was the perfect temperature. I glided through the water, enjoying the feeling of weightlessness, of freedom. As I reached the other side of the pool mid-way down the length of it, she joined me.

We treaded water for a few moments, enjoying the gentle night breeze. Camille tilted her head back, her gaze drifting toward the velvety black sky. She sighed contentedly.

"Nate and I fell in love right here at this resort," she said, her voice soft. "It's hard to believe it's only been a few months."

"I can see why," I replied, gazing around at the serene, tropical setting. "This place is amazing. It would be the perfect place to fall in love."

Camille smiled. "It was pretty magical. Though it took a while for us to get there."

"Clay and Nate are close," I said, thinking about the easy banter I'd witnessed between them since I started working for Clay. Nate had an ability to get him to open up like few others did. "It's nice that they have such a strong bond."

Camille nodded. "They've always had each other's

backs, even when they were driving each other crazy. Like most brothers, I guess."

"You must know them both really well," I observed, thinking about how little I actually knew about Clay outside of his work persona.

Camille laughed. "I do! I practically grew up with them. My childhood home is right next door to the Harmons in Westport, Connecticut. Nate and I are spending a lot of time there now. Getting the place fixed up."

"That sounds nice," I said, picturing a cozy New England farmhouse. A stark contrast to Clay's sleek Manhattan penthouse, which I'd never seen but could just imagine.

"It's definitely no tropical paradise," Camille replied, her grin widening. "But it feels like home. And being close to Nate's family is important to both of us."

We fell silent for a moment, enjoying the night's warmth and the gentle sway of the water.

"This whole sale has been pretty stressful," I said, sweeping my arms in broad strokes as I treaded water. "Podium is a huge success. Clay has been working nonstop for months preparing."

Camille leaned back against the wall, tall enough to stand up. "I'm sure he has. This whole Podium thing has been Clay's obsession for years. And he never does anything halfway. But he surprised me tonight." She tilted her head, studying me with a playful glint in her eyes. "It's nice to see him taking a break from work. I have a hard time picturing Clay Harmon scuba diving."

The vision of Clay's bare, chiseled chest on the dive boat floated through my mind. I let my eyes unfocus, allowing myself to savor the image.

Then Camille's voice brought me back to earth. "I thought he was going to turn this place into a 24-hour boardroom. But at dinner, he was surprisingly... chill."

I laughed. "You should have seen him in action this morning during our session with the two bidders. That was pure Clay Harmon, laser-focused and ready to take on the world."

Smiling, Camille nodded sagely. "Oh, I have no doubt about that. He's definitely got the killer instinct. Though he seems to be doing a better job here of letting go." She paused, her gaze meeting mine. "Maybe someone's having a particular effect on him."

Heat crept up my neck, and I shifted to hook my elbow on the pool deck, letting my legs float to the surface. "He's just enjoying the vacation atmosphere, I guess." I kept my voice even, trying to sound nonchalant even as I thought of that magnetic pull between us last night at dinner. And again this evening.

Camille's eyebrows shot up, a mischievous grin spreading across her face as she glanced at the cottage. "Vacation atmosphere, huh? Looks like you two are sharing quite a bit of that atmosphere."

"It's not like that," I replied quickly. Trying to deny that it was exactly like that. "Clay brought me here because my room had a plumbing issue. They couldn't fix it, and the resort is booked, so Clay offered me his spare room."

Camille burst out laughing. The sound echoed across the water, mingling with the gentle lapping of waves against the pool's edge. "Oh, please. That sounds like something out of a romance novel! The billionaire CEO sharing his luxurious cottage with his beautiful assistant." She leaned in conspiratorially, lowering her voice. "You've worked for him for a while now, but I wouldn't blame you if you were just a tiny bit starstruck. He has quite the aura about him."

My cheeks burned even hotter, and I was grateful for the dim lighting around the pool. "It's not... I mean, we're just—" I stammered, searching for the right words. "Clay's my boss, Camille. It's strictly professional."

Camille's grin remained as she lifted her legs to float lazily onto her back, her yellow bikini a vibrant contrast against the turquoise pool lit with hidden spotlights. "Uh-huh. Strictly professional. That's why you're blushing like a schoolgirl right now."

I splashed water in her direction playfully, trying to deflect. "Oh, stop it. You're imagining things."

"Am I?"

I decided to go on offense. "You're the one who is dating the pro hockey player and billionaire. Maybe you're seeing echoes of your own story."

Camille laughed softly, tipping upright to dance her fingers over the water's surface. "Touché. Though Nate was a real challenge," she continued, her voice taking on a more serious tone. She flipped onto her stomach, treading water as she faced me. "Turning that playboy around was no easy feat. But you don't need to worry about that with Clay. He's never been a tomcat. Or a weirdo boss who goes after his employees, for that matter."

A chill ran through me, despite the warm water, as the memory of Burt coming onto me flashed through my mind. I shuddered involuntarily but kept the incident to myself. Clay was different, and Camille just reinforced that.

"You okay?" she asked, noticing my momentary discomfort.

I nodded quickly, forcing a smile. "Just a little chill. Go on."

Camille's eyes softened, and she moved closer. "If you and Clay do end up together, you'll hopefully have an easier time of it than Nate and I did."

My forced smile turned into a completely genuine laugh. The idea was absurd, no matter how my heart fluttered at the thought. "There's zero chance of that happening," I insisted, pushing off from the pool's edge to float on my back. The stars above seemed to mock me with their twinkling brilliance. "Nothing with Clay is ever simple."

"He's a complicated guy. Not going to argue that. My Harmon is the more straightforward one. And the more attractive Harmon, if you want my opinion," she added with a teasing lilt.

I disagreed but kept silent.

As if on cue, the sliding glass door opened with a soft whoosh. Nate's silhouette appeared, backlit by the warm illumination from inside the cottage.

"Hey, gorgeous," he called out, his voice filled with affection and anticipation. "You about ready to head out? I've got some plans for us back at our place. Private plans."

Camille's eyes lit up. She giggled, the sound light and flirtatious. "Ooh, I've been waiting all night to hear that." In one fluid motion, she hoisted herself out of the pool, water cascading off her toned body.

I watched as she sauntered over to Nate, grabbing a towel and her beach bag on the way. He wrapped an arm around her waist, pulling her close despite her damp skin. He whispered something to her, eliciting more laughing from Camille.

"Night, Elise!" she called over her shoulder as they strolled off with their arms around each other. "Don't stay up too late!"

"Night, you two," I replied, waving from the pool. "See you tomorrow!"

As they faded into the distance, I found myself smiling. Their easy affection was sweet, and a little enviable. But as the silence settled around me, broken only by the gentle lapping of water against the pool's edge, my smile faded.

My thoughts drifted to Clay. What was he was doing inside right now? Working? Planning his next move, strategizing for tomorrow's meetings? Always three steps ahead, always in control.

And yet... Camille didn't seem to think the idea of Clay and me together was so far-fetched. She knew him better than I did, had known him for years.

Is it possible she sees something I can't?

I shook my head, trying to clear away the dangerous thoughts. Entertaining such ideas would only lead to disappointment and complications. Still, a small part of me couldn't help but wonder...

With a sigh, I turned over in the water, stretching out into a lazy freestyle stroke. The cool water slid over my skin as I glided through it, my movements slow and purposeful. As I swam, I tried to focus on the physical sensation, on the peacefulness of the night around me. But even as I completed my lap, my mind kept circling back to Clay, to possibilities I shouldn't even be considering.

I was so lost in thought that I barely noticed the soft sound of the patio door sliding open. As I lifted my head from the water, I caught sight of a figure on the deck. Clay stood motionless on the deck watching me. My stomach lurched, but that was quickly replaced by a surge of excitement rushing through me.

Until I remembered what I was wearing.

I hadn't planned on him seeing me in this string bikini.

And now that he was here, I wasn't quite sure how to handle the situation. I swam to the pool's edge and climbed out, hyper-aware of Clay's gaze on me. His eyes were riveted to me, lingering on my breasts before dropping to my feet then slowly, slowly back up. Droplets of water ran down my skin as I approached him, and at his hungry expression, my self-consciousness threatened to become replaced by a thrilling boldness.

"Hi there," I said, my voice huskier than usual as I grabbed a towel to cover up. "I thought you were staying inside."

"Here, let me help you," Clay said, his deep voice striking something deep within me. He strode toward me and took the towel from my hand. His action was confident and bold, the movement of a man used to being obeyed. And the thought of being the object of his desire was irresistible. As he held the towel open, his eyes met mine. "Though I think it's an absolute crime to cover up such a spectacular body."

Heat flooded my body at his words. "It was my only suit that was dry," I replied, holding his gaze with newfound confidence.

Then I felt the soft terrycloth on my shoulder, and soon he trailed it down my arm. My skin tingled at the touch, and I deliberately leaned into him, drawn by an irresistible pull. I wanted him to touch me—to hell with the consequences.

"You look beautiful in the moonlight," he said softly.

As our eyes met again, the air between us crackled with electricity.

I opened my mouth to reply, but my response was captured by his mouth. Our lips met, and I couldn't prevent the breathy moan that issued from my lungs. His kiss deepened, and I pressed against him eagerly, my damp skin warming rapidly under his touch. The towel fell away, forgotten.

"Clay..." I sighed, running my hands up his shirt to grip his shoulders.

His tongue parted my lips, and I responded hungrily, clutching at the fabric of his shirt and pulling him closer. Our tongues danced as his hands moved to my ass, squeezing and pressing me against him. I could feel his arousal, and it only fueled my own desire.

Caught up in the moment, I nipped at his bottom lip, delighting in his groan of pleasure. He tangled one hand in my wet hair, tugging gently as he deepened the kiss further. I arched into him, my body aflame.

Just as I was losing myself completely, Clay stiffened and pulled away. His eyes flew open wide, and he breathed hard as he took a giant step back. "Elise, I... I'm sorry."

Confusion and disappointment washed over me, and my body still thrummed with desire. "It's okay."

"No, it's not. I shouldn't have done that. Good night." With that, Clay spun around and strode back to the house, leaving me standing alone by the pool, my skin flushed and my hands trembling.

I wrapped my arms around myself, my mind reeling. What had just happened? And why had it ended so abruptly? As I watched Clay's stiff, retreating form, my confusion only deepened. The passion between us had been undeniable, but now I was left wondering if I'd just crossed a line that couldn't be uncrossed.

Chapter Fourteen

Clay

MUSTERING every ounce of self-control I possessed, I marched through the living room and retreated to my bedroom, leaving Elise standing by the pool. Shutting the door, I leaned against it and closed my eyes.

"This is what I get for listening to Nate. Dick."

After he and Camille left, I'd gone outside and been utterly transfixed by the sight of Elise in that red bikini—it had blown my fantasies to smithereens. And before I knew it, I'd been unable to stop myself from kissing her. Then kissing her more. Deeper. I couldn't get enough. Thank God I'd come to my senses in time.

As I leaned against the door, I was tormented. I brushed my fingers lightly over my lips, remembering her soft, wet tongue and how her body had melted against mine. Attraction warred with responsibility as I stripped off my clothes and stepped into the freezing spray of the shower. The icy water did little to quell the fire burning within me, but it gave me time to think. I wanted nothing more than to march across the cottage to her room and make her scream my name.

But that couldn't happen.

I might be an asshole. Hell, I was an asshole. But not that kind. I wasn't a predator.

So instead, I climbed into my bed.

Alone.

Horny.

Miserable.

And with a strong sense that I wasn't making the right decision here. But I *couldn't* let anything happen between us. Yet as sleep claimed me, my last thought was of that breathtaking, unforgettable kiss.

I WOKE UP EARLY, before it was fully light. How the hell was I going to backpedal from this? We couldn't just pretend like that kiss never happened, but I didn't know what to do now. And I didn't want her thinking I was a cold, aloof prick. I was becoming very aware I hadn't treated her well over the past three years.

Appreciated her as an assistant and part of my empire, yes.

But now I was seeing *her*. The very desirable, intelligent woman.

I couldn't allow us to cross that line again, especially not after what she experienced with Bart. But maybe we could form a new baseline. After dressing in casual drawstring pants and a T-shirt, I called room service to have a light breakfast delivered. In the living room, I tried not to pace as I waited for her to emerge from her bedroom.

I poured some coffee to distract myself. We were diving again this afternoon, but my morning was completely open.

I'd seen a stack of paddleboards and kayaks on the beach and a smile raised my lips. Kayaking and exploring the island might be just the thing to get my mind off Elise.

I heard the door open, and an entire flock of nerves took off in my stomach. It was an unusual sensation and one I didn't like, which only reinforced that I needed to make things right between us.

Elise moved hesitantly across the floor. She was dressed in shorts and a pretty blouse, and her hair was coiled into a messy bun.

A lock of hair had fallen over my forehead, and I swept it back. "Morning. Coffee?"

"Please," she replied, taking a seat in an armchair adjacent to me as I handed her a steaming cup. She wrapped both hands around it and took a long inhale, giving me a tentative smile.

"Listen," I said, diving in. "About last night... I want to apologize again for kissing you. After what you went through with Bart, that was the last thing you need to deal with. It was a lapse in judgment, and I hope you'll forgive me."

"Of course," she said quickly, her throat bobbing as she swallowed. And an emotion flickered through her eyes, something I couldn't quite decipher before it was gone. Could it have been disappointment? Then she nodded firmly. "We just got a little swept up in the tropical night. Let's just forget about it."

"Agreed," I said crisply, and realized I sounded like her boss again. Dammit. "I, uh, ordered us both breakfast."

A smile graced her face as she surveyed the yogurt, granola, and fresh tropical fruit, and spooned some of each into her bowl. "Thanks. It looks delicious."

As I started with my own breakfast, I searched for something to say. A way to connect. And I realized I knew almost nothing about the woman sitting next to me. How was that possible? "You know, I don't even know where you live in the city."

She took a sip of coffee and barked a laugh. "Queens. It's not much, but I can afford my own place. And that's because you pay me well. Thank you for that."

I thought of my four-thousand square-foot penthouse apartment overlooking Central Park and felt like a complete dick. And I didn't want any reminders that I was her boss. "You've more than earned it. What do you do outside work?"

She gave me a long, even stare, like she understood perfectly that I was only now realizing that I didn't know much about her. "Night school has taken up most of my spare time. But now that I've graduated, I've joined a gym and I'm taking painting classes."

I grinned. "You have a creative streak?"

She laughed and a beautiful flush crossed her face. "I don't know about that. My paintings so far have been pretty awful."

"Still, at least it's something. I usually exercise in the evenings, or just continue working until I go to bed. Maybe I should join you in that painting class." Which might have been the most idiotic sentence I had ever uttered. Nate would be on the floor laughing if he'd heard it.

But Elise just smiled broadly, as if she found the idea charming. "I'll save you a spot at the next class, then."

We continued to chat over breakfast. I found out she was an only child, and a shadow crossed her face when she talked about her parents, but she quickly smiled again as she told me she graduated top of her class.

When we were on the last of the coffee, her eye fell on

my appointment book sitting on the coffee table. "Your schedule is clear until our dive with Nate and Camille later. Any plans?"

Coffee cup in hand, I sat back against the couch. "Yes. Nate is meeting again with Laurent and Celeste this morning without me. I was thinking of checking out a kayak from the kiosk on the beach and exploring the wetland area to the north. Just to get my mind off the sale for a while. And the decision. How about you?"

Her lips curved into a lush smile, and I tried not to stare at her mouth. "That's funny. I looked outside after I got up and had a similar thought. It's such a beautiful morning, too lovely to spend indoors."

My stomach tightened as I thought about what her lips had tasted like. With effort, I wrenched my eyes to hers. And that current was back. That delicious push and pull between us at the fact that we had independently decided to do the exact same thing.

Before I could think about it, I opened my mouth. "Would you like to join me?"

The idea was either fantastic or terrible, and I couldn't decide which. But I wanted to spend time with her—I liked hearing her laugh. I wanted to know her better.

She hesitated for a moment, then inclined her head. "That sounds like fun. Let's finish breakfast, then head out."

As I refilled our coffee cups, I again pondered how wise this was. I thrived on control, on strong boundaries and high moral ground. So what was it about this woman that made me want to throw all that to the wind and just let go?

Chapter Fifteen

Elise

AFTER WE FINISHED BREAKFAST, Clay and I retreated to our bedrooms to get ready for our paddling trip. I felt dazed as I walked into my bedroom and shut the door, hardly able to remember leaving the living room. The range of emotions I'd experienced this morning left me numb as I tried to process them. Waking up this morning and being terrified of confronting Clay. Then seeing his genuine regret and worry, I'd felt...

How did I feel?

Everything he'd said made sense. He had a deep core of honor inside him—I'd always known that. Clay Harmon and I as a couple? Ridiculous. And dammit, I appreciated his integrity in stepping back, even if it made me want to smack him. And there were some huge risks here for me too.

I was so confused about it all, but my God, who knew he'd be such a good kisser! I needed to clear my head over what had happened and how to proceed. So I grabbed my phone and called as I flopped back onto my bed.

"Hey, girl! How's life in paradise?" Rachel's cheerful voice rang through the speaker.

"Good morning!" I replied, trying to sound upbeat. "Everything is going smoothly. The Podium sale is on track, and we're finalizing plans for the gala tomorrow night." Silence followed, and I could almost see Rachel raising an eyebrow.

"How lovely," she drawled, clearly not buying it. "Now why are you really calling?"

I laughed, unable to help it. "Okay, you got me. I just... um... I kissed Clay last night, and I'm freaking out. Clay!" I said in a stage-whisper as I attempted to keep my voice down.

"Wow. Really? Okay, first of all, congratulations on finally getting some action. He obviously learned you're not a piece of furniture."

"Oh, yeah."

"Well, how was it? Did he kiss like a robot?"

A long, hot roll rounded over my abdomen. It was rich and buttery. "It was the best kiss I've ever had in my life. And that's not a good thing, Rach!"

She sighed. "Seriously, why are you so worried? You two are both grown adults. Why not have a little fun in the tropics?"

I bolted upright and dragged a hand through my tangled hair. "Because if this goes badly, I might end up having to find a new job! After the sale, I'm hoping to transition to something new within the company. I'm counting on that being a huge career move."

"Sweetie, if you're romantically involved with Clay Harmon, that might *really* be your big move."

"Ugh, thanks for pointing that out," I grumbled, frowning. "I've seen some of the gold diggers he's been involved with. I'm not interested in his money. Or his power. I'm attracted to him."

"Who wouldn't be? He is rather amazing looking."

"And it's more than that. I... *like* him. I've discovered this whole other side of him since we've been here. A fun, human side. I don't want him thinking I'm looking for a meal ticket or something."

"You've always been too independent for your own good. Don't make a molehill into the Himalayas! Go with the flow, have a fun fling, and reevaluate when you get back to New York. Life's too short for regrets."

I sighed. The part of me that wanted to jump Clay's bones this very minute was arguing with my very rational and down-to-earth brain. "Well, there's not just me to be concerned about. He put a stop to it last night, then he apologized again this morning. We talked through it and are back on solid footing again." I frowned. "At least I think we are."

"Ah, I see. The two type-A, driven personalities let their logical sides take over and made a very practical decision to step back from disaster."

"Jeez, now you're making me sound like a robot!"

She burst into laughter. "Honestly, from what you just told me, I think you two might just be perfect for each other. Obviously the man has a moral compass, and he's proven there's a human being hiding inside him too. Maybe you two just need to relax and let nature take its course."

"I just don't want things to get really weird between us. I'll let you know how it goes." I told her about our plans to go kayaking. "But just as two people enjoying the morning. Nothing else."

"I'm just saying that for once in your life, maybe you should let go, Elise! But at any rate, go enjoy that tropical paradise. Relax and have some fun. Bonus points if that fun involves a certain tall, dark, and handsome billionaire. Love you!"

A smile remained on my face as I returned the sentiment before ending the call. And maybe my feet had a little extra bounce as I walked to change into board shorts and a rash guard.

Rachel was right. Clay and I had quickly gotten over the awkwardness and now something new was starting. He'd actually asked about me as a person! Minutes later, he and I walked along the stunning white beach together toward the kayak and paddleboard kiosk.

"I think I'll stick with a kayak," I said. "I'm not sure a paddleboard and I would be a good combination." It was more that I didn't want to look like an idiot and fall off in front of him, which was a very high probability.

"I prefer kayaks too," he replied.

Clay and I checked out our kayaks and he helped me into mine. Together we set off on the gentle ocean, heading north toward the mangrove area the kiosk attendant recommended as a great place to explore. I was a little awkward at first, but I quickly found a relaxing rhythm as I paddled on one side, then the other. We passed the pale-pink Orchid restaurant, silent in the morning light.

A short distance later, the manicured resort grounds gave way to arching trees with trunks and roots sunk into the brackish water. "Here we are," Clay said as we headed toward a broad, watery tunnel ahead. Tall, green trees arched overhead, and the area had a leafy, rich scent. "Ready?"

"Definitely," I replied, smiling back at him as I dipped my paddle into the still water.

We glided together through the breathtaking marsh, sunlight filtering through the dense foliage above us and casting dappled patterns on the water. It was magical, like something out of a dream. Ospreys nested in the taller trees, their keen eyes watching us from above, while white egrets flew gracefully overhead. At one point, we even spotted a manatee lazily swimming in the distance.

"This is amazing," I murmured, unable to tear my eyes away from the vibrant world around us.

Clay nodded. "I loved exploring this place when I was a kid. There's always something new to discover."

As we continued to paddle, I found myself sneaking glances at Clay. He seemed so at ease here, so different from the laser-focused businessman I knew back in New York. A sleeveless shirt showed every muscle of his arms flexing as he paddled.

"Look!" Clay pointed at something up ahead. A turtle was sunning itself on a fallen tree trunk, its head stretched toward the sky. It was a peaceful scene that somehow made the moment between us feel even more intimate.

"He's a big guy," I murmured, the sight captivating me.

The reptile turned its head to regard us but otherwise remained still. Our kayaks drifted closer together, our paddles momentarily forgotten. My pulse quickened as I met Clay's gaze, feeling that familiar spark between us. He stared back at me, his eyes filled with a heat that had nothing to do with proper workplace behavior.

I was so entranced by the moment that I didn't notice my kayak drifting toward Clay's until we collided with a bump. Our laughter broke the silence, and the turtle dove back into the water with a splash.

"Sorry." I giggled as we got our wobbling kayaks under control again. "I guess I got a little distracted."

"That's okay." Clay's smile lingered. That damn lock of hair flopped over his forehead again and he casually swept it back. "Have you ever been kayaking before?"

"No," I admitted, a bit embarrassed as I started paddling again. "I grew up near a river in Pennsylvania, but I never spent much time on it."

"Really?" Clay asked curiously. "Well, you're doing great for a first-timer."

"Thanks," I replied, trying to brush off the compliment despite the glow spreading through me at his praise. "How about you? You seem pretty comfortable in a kayak. Do you do this often?"

He shrugged, a trace of sheepishness tingeing his handsome features as we moved through a broad canal. "Not exactly kayaking, but I was on the crew team at Harvard. It's not quite the same thing, but it's close enough. Though I haven't done much of anything outside the gym in years. I'd forgotten how peaceful it is to be on the water." His face clouded as he followed the movement of a massive blue heron gliding silently just over the water.

Two years ago, a leading sports magazine wrote a feature on Clay and Nate. They both stood on the cover, Clay in a suit and Nate in his New York Rangers jersey, both unsmiling and unbelievably gorgeous. Even back then, my gaze had repeatedly slid back to the icy blue eyes of my boss. Inside, I'd discovered that Clay's journey to Harvard wasn't unlike my own to Penn State. He was the valedictorian of his New England high school class and earned a full-ride scholarship. Just like I did. Our paths diverged there, however. I earned a bachelor's in business but had been equally interested in hanging out with my friends. At Harvard, he made the business contacts he would use to build his empire.

I glanced at his serious face as we paddled under a low-hanging branch. Apparently, that empire had come at more of a personal cost than I'd realized. I was glad he was taking time to enjoy our respite.

"I can understand why you have such fond memories of Calypso Key," I said, sighing as I took in the lush scenery. "It's such a beautiful, tranquil place."

A smile spread across Clay's face, making my heart skip a beat. "Yeah, Nate and I used to spend hours exploring this mangrove when we were kids. One time, our mother even sent the resort staff to find us when we lost track of time."

As he shared the story, I pictured a young Clay and Nate, full of adventure and wonder as they navigated these waters. Had he been a happy, carefree child? Or serious and determined? He hadn't grown up rich. His family had been solidly upper-middle class.

His grin faded as he stared at the horizon. "I've let too much of life slip away. I've been so busy with the business, I never even noticed."

And I was more than an ambitious woman in a business skirt, but had I forgotten that? How long had it been since I'd just strolled in the park a block from my apartment? "Maybe we could all use a reminder to slow down and enjoy the simple things in life."

"Maybe you're right," he agreed, his blue eyes once again meeting mine.

And once again I couldn't look away.

Time stilled as we floated, our kayaks gently rocking in the current. The air between us grew thick, and the memory of how his mouth had tasted rushed back. Heat flared through me.

As if sensing my thoughts, Clay cleared his throat and looked away. "We should probably head back."

"Right," I replied, blinking. "Back to reality."

We turned our kayaks around and paddled back toward the resort, but the atmosphere between us had shifted. I stole glances at Clay as we moved through the water, admiring his broad shoulders and toned muscles. The man could wear a suit like it was a second skin, but seeing him in casual attire, a simple white shirt and khaki shorts, made me appreciate what lay beneath his polished exterior.

"Elise," he called out, breaking my reverie. "Watch that tree root!"

Squeaking, I jabbed my paddle out and pushed off the gnarled wood. I'd been staring and totally lost track of where I was. Fortunately, he hadn't seemed to notice. "Yeah, just lost in thought."

"About what?" he asked, a hint of curiosity in his voice.

"Life, I guess," I said, thinking fast. I hesitated before continuing, studying the placid water with its flitting movement of fish beneath. "I've been so focused on my career that I kind of forgot how to live too. This is actually the first time I've been out of the city in two years, except for quick visits to my parents." And those visits had presented their own challenges, serving as a reminder of why I'd left Pennsylvania in the first place. Especially Christmas visits. But I hadn't exactly made it a priority to explore the Big Apple, despite living in it.

"Two years? That's a long time to be stuck in the concrete jungle."

"I know," I said, smiling ruefully. "But being here has

made me aware there's more to life than work. And maybe I need to find some balance."

He nodded. "That's something we could both work on, then."

"Deal." I grinned at him, still surprised at this new sense of camaraderie between us. It was heartening to know that even someone as successful as Clay struggled with finding balance.

As we approached the resort, our conversation continued to flow easily. Though we'd known each other for years, it felt like I was getting a rare glimpse of the man beneath the suit. The real Clay Harmon.

"Thanks for inviting me along this morning," I told him as we pulled our kayaks onto the beach. "It was exactly what I needed."

"Likewise," he replied, his eyes meeting mine. "This trip has been... unexpected."

"In a good way, I hope."

"Yes. As you said, simple pleasures. Seeing things in a new light. I enjoyed our kayaking a lot."

"Maybe we can do it again before we leave," I suggested, my heartbeat quickening at the thought.

"I'd like that."

As we walked back to the cottage, that same sense of excitement and apprehension filled me about what lay ahead. Since Clay and I had come to Florida, our connection had changed.

We were more than boss and assistant now.

As we'd paddled along, I hadn't been the only one stealing glances. Clay saw me as a woman, likely for the first time ever. But could we truly forget who we were and give in to this new connection between us?

Clay frowned and plucked at his sleeveless shirt as we

neared the cottage. "Let's cool off in the pool before we meet Nate and Camille."

"Excellent idea."

My skin was sticky from the humid air, and a dip in the pool would be just the thing to refresh me. But as I retreated to my room to change, I hesitated between my modest one-piece swimsuit and a more daring dark-red bikini. After a moment's thought, I decided on the bikini. He'd noticed me in it last night. Why not embrace my newfound confidence?

As I emerged from my room, Clay was already treading water in the pool. His gaze was riveted on me as I padded across the deck. A surge of energy hummed through me, as if I were stepping into a new life instead of across a pool deck. Slowly, I walked down the stairs into the water, submerging myself and swimming gracefully along the length of the pool. The sensation of cool water rushing over my skin was thrilling, heightening every sensation I was feeling. I rose to the surface to stand in shoulder-deep water. I felt sensuous, exotic, and raised both arms to sweep my wet hair back.

Clay waded over, stopping to face me. "Diving, paddling, and now swimming. I didn't know you were so athletic."

"I wouldn't go that far," I said, laughing lightly. "But I guess we're both full of surprises today."

"Indeed," he agreed, his eyes dropping to my breasts before rising to my face again.

I rested my elbow on the pool deck and relaxed. "Has Calypso Key changed since you were here last?"

"God, yes. Back then it was a lot more rustic." His grin sent another hot jolt through me. "Just perfect for two young boys wanting to explore. But I prefer it more as it is now. As a man, I've developed a taste for the finer things in life." Those pale eyes held mine as he said those words, and I inhaled deeply, suddenly finding the air starved of oxygen.

"Just don't forget about the simple pleasures too," I told him. "Like spending a morning on the water, surrounded by nature."

"True," he agreed, taking a step closer. "Some moments are worth savoring, even if they're fleeting."

As I stared at him, my pulse quickened, and the water around us seemed to become electric. Fire burned in his pale blue gaze, a heat that mirrored the desire welling within me. My insides turned to molten liquid as I became aware of the throbbing sensation between my legs. My eyes dropped to his full, inviting lips, and I reached out the tip of my tongue to touch my bottom lip without thinking about it.

Clay's rough, strained voice broke through the silence. "Oh, to hell with responsibility."

In an instant, he grabbed me by the shoulders and pulled me in, crushing his mouth against mine. We fell together, standing in the pool, our passion igniting. I matched his intensity, our kiss lengthening and deepening with every passing second. Everywhere he touched left me scorching, and every stroke of his fingers made me yearn for more.

My hands roamed over his broad, slick back, the muscles rippling beneath my fingertips as I groaned against his mouth. He murmured into the kiss, telling me how much he wanted me. I reached down and palmed him over his board shorts, feeling his hardness, the undeniable proof of his desire for me. His hand found my breast and cupped it, sending shivers down my spine.

"Clay," I gasped, pulling back from his mouth to stare at him. "I don't want to stop. Let's forget who we are. Right now, we're just a woman and a man who want each other."

His eyes flicked away from mine for a moment, scanning the beach in front of the pool as if suddenly aware of our surroundings. "Let's go inside where it's private."

Without another word, he kissed me again—a hard, raking kiss that seared through me and made my legs wobble—before scooping me up into his arms and carrying me out of the pool and into the cottage.

Chapter Sixteen

Clay

I CARRIED Elise into my bedroom as she laid a trail of kisses across my neck. Every one shot straight through me. Once inside, I set her down. My eyes locked onto hers, and I was helpless to resist the electric connection racing between us.

Without speaking, I grabbed her face with both hands, pulling her into a scorching kiss that sent shockwaves throughout my entire body. I claimed her mouth, completely unable to think of anything else but having her right there and then.

"Oh, Clay." Elise panted when we broke apart for a brief moment, her wet hair tousled around her head, making her look utterly gorgeous and wild in a way I'd never seen before.

"You have no idea how much you turn me on," I breathed, my voice barely audible as I pushed her against the wall, my hands roaming her body as I deepened the kiss.

The feel of her soft skin under my fingertips only fueled my need for her. "You're driving me absolutely insane."

"Good," she replied breathlessly, "because I can't get enough of you either."

My heart pounded as I trapped her against the wall with my body, our mouths locked together in a fiery dance. "Elise," I murmured against her lips, my voice deep and husky. "I want to explore every inch of you, to learn all your secrets. I want to make you *mine*."

"Then what are you waiting for?" Her eyes were dark and full of invitation.

And with those words, any last shred of self-control I had left vanished.

Elise responded hungrily to my touch. Her hands gripped my shoulders as she matched my intensity, her tongue plunging into my mouth.

"Since the moment I saw you in that bikini last night," I told her, my voice rough and strained, "I've wanted to rip it off."

And without hesitation, I did just that, untying her bikini top and ripping it off, exposing her beautiful breasts to my gaze. My hands immediately found them, squeezing hard, and she responded with a breathy moan.

"Your turn," she said, her voice sultry, and before I knew it, she had torn my shirt off. Our bare torsos came together, the sensation of her soft skin against my chest sending wave after wave of heat through me.

Her warm hands slid my board shorts off my hips, and she sank to her knees. She opened her soft lips to take me in, sucking gently. I groaned as I watched her movements, her lips drawing me in and out.

"You're so beautiful like that." My voice was thick with desire as I gathered her hair in one hand to see her better.

Her eyes crinkled in a smile, holding my gaze without disturbing her rhythm. It was the most erotic thing I'd ever seen. My body trembled with anticipation, every fiber of my being focused on the pleasure she was giving me. As she kneeled before me, her warm mouth enveloping me, my world narrowed down to this single, breathtaking moment. I was breathing hard through my mouth, and I let go to stroke one hand through her wet strands. All that mattered was her and what she was doing to me.

I didn't want it to end so soon. I wanted to make her completely unable to form words. Except my name. That I wanted to hear.

"Wait," I gasped, my entire body trembling on the edge of release. Elise glanced up at me, her lips still wrapped around me, her eyes questioning but filled with desire.

"Stand up," I commanded, feeling a surge of power and control as I stepped back and pulled her to her feet. My hands grasped hers, leading her to the bed. I ripped off her bikini bottoms in a frenzy, discarding them like an afterthought as our lips met, kissing deeply, tongues dancing together.

After ripping back the covers, I pushed her back onto the bed, my body following closely behind. As I crawled over her, my eyes locked onto her sex. Without hesitation, I dove in, swirling and tasting as my hands roamed over her body. I gripped her breasts, then slid my hands down to grab her bucking hips.

"Yes!" she moaned, her voice breathless and filled with want. Her fingers tangled in my hair, pulling me closer. Her body arched toward my mouth, seeking more contact. She was so close.

"Please, Clay," she begged, her voice barely more than a whisper.

I grunted, my mouth never leaving her as I doubled my efforts. Her hips bucked wildly despite me gripping them hard enough to leave indentations on her skin. Then she screamed, my name falling from her lips like a prayer as she experienced what sounded like an earth-shattering orgasm. Her body shook beneath mine, her hips freezing as waves of pleasure washed over her.

Driven by my own desire and the effect she had on me, I reached for the nightstand drawer and my wallet. My fingers found a condom, and I quickly tore open the package and rolled it on. Her gaze was locked onto mine, filled with hunger and anticipation. She licked her lips and my whole body twitched.

As I positioned myself above her, the air between us crackled. Our bodies were like magnets, pulling together with irresistible force. I slammed into her, and she gasped at the sudden contact, her legs wrapping around my waist, drawing me even deeper inside her.

"My God, you feel incredible," I groaned as I pounded into her again and again. Our bodies moved in perfect sync, our passion building with every thrust. The bed creaked beneath us, but neither of us cared. I wasn't capable of conscious thought at this point. My entire existence narrowed to the sensations rocketing through me. Building. The heat of her body beneath mine. I lost myself in her, something I never did.

I never gave up control.

But this felt so good. So right. Elise's nails raked over my ass, sending a jolt of pain mingling with pleasure straight through me. I hissed at the sensation, driving into her with more fervor.

"More, Clay. Harder. Deeper," she groaned into my ear, her voice desperate and needy.

"Oh, yes," I promised, my own desire spiraling out of control. I sucked her neck hard, leaving a red mark. "You have no idea what you do to me."

"Show me," she whispered against my ear. The soft air sent another jolt through me, edging me ever closer. "Show me how much you want me."

That was all the encouragement I needed. With a guttural growl, I increased the intensity of my thrusts, determined to drive her to the very brink. I pounded into her with abandon, the pressure building inside me, that familiar coil of pleasure tightening until it threatened to snap. Yet unfamiliar—stronger, more urgent. Sliding one hand behind her, I gripped one velvety cheek, pushing us even closer together. Elise closed her eyes, gripping me tightly as she cried out with her own release, urging me on.

"My God," I choked out, my body finally succumbing to the overwhelming pleasure as I experienced the most powerful climax of my life. It was raw, consuming, and unlike anything I had ever felt before—an explosion of ecstasy that left me breathless and reeling.

Exhausted and breathless, I collapsed, our bodies intertwined like vines clinging to each other in the aftermath of a storm. The room echoed with our ragged breathing.

As I slowly came back to myself, concern rose. "Are you all right?"

She nodded against my neck, her breaths still coming in short gasps. "Yes. That was . . . I'm not sure what that was. But I am much more than all right."

I laughed softly, relief rolling through me as I ran a hand through her messy, still wet, hair. "I'm sorry if I was too rough. I don't usually lose control like that."

Elise shifted her head, her eyes meeting mine with a mischievous glint. "It's nice to see you let loose. Besides, I think we both lost control," she said, her voice a mixture of amusement and satisfaction. "It was wonderful."

Rolling off her and onto my back, I took her with me. I wrapped my arms around her, her skin damp against mine. As I held her, her breathing began to slow, deepening as she started to drift off.

"Clay," Elise murmured, her words muffled against my chest.

"Yeah?" I replied, tracing my fingers over her back.

"Thank you," she whispered. "For not holding back. For letting go with me."

I pressed a kiss to her hair, closing my eyes at the sense of fulfillment that seemed to radiate from every fiber of my being. How strange it was, this feeling that welled up inside me. I'd always prided myself on maintaining control, especially when it came to matters of the heart. I usually preferred to sleep alone, finding someone near irritating, but now I couldn't imagine letting go of the woman in my arms. And it was broad daylight.

"Is losing control a good thing or a bad thing?" I wondered aloud.

"Sometimes," Elise murmured, her eyes closed as she nestled closer to me. "It's the only way to find ourselves."

And with a contented sigh, Elise pressed closer. I held her tighter and breathed a long, contented sigh. I fell asleep instantly.

Chapter Seventeen

Elise

SHARK BAIT slowly motored out of the canal, then quickly picked up speed after we reached open water. A smile was etched on my face at the thought of exploring the under-water world once more. Though it *was* possible that the smile had more to do with other things I wanted to explore more of. I sighed as a slight tremor rippled through me and avoided looking at Clay. Just to prove I could do it.

Nate and Camille buzzed with anticipation as they secured their diving gear. Like last time, we were on a private trip, this time with Maia Markham-Taylor guiding us. The youngest of the Markham children, she was firmly ensconced in the family business, though she couldn't have been out of her twenties. I glanced at Clay across the boat, and our eyes locked for a moment. Heat flooded my face as our morning came rushing back to me. We had stayed in bed until it was time to leave on the dive trip, and I couldn't wait to be alone with him again. To distract myself, I checked my own gear to make sure all was in order. When I stood back up, he was right next to me.

"Ready?" he asked, breathing the word in my ear.

"Ready for anything," I replied. I hadn't been sure how Clay would react now that Nate and Camille were with us. But he was one hundred percent Casual Clay now, laughing with his hair windswept and messy. Though not overt in his interest toward me, he wasn't hiding it either.

At my reply, he favored me with a smile that made my insides melt. "Hold that thought until later, then. Let's go dive."

We plunged into the water. Schools of fish darted around us, their vibrant colors shimmering as they swam past coral formations that seemed to reach out like welcoming arms. I felt absolutely free, untethered from the world above.

As we descended deeper, Clay stayed by my side. Every so often, his hand would brush against mine, sending tingles up my spine even in the warm water. Because this time they weren't errant, accidental touches. The familiar tension between us never waned, even as we were caught up in the wonders surrounding us.

Maia led us along a sheer wall, plunging into the depths. Looking down, I felt a little dizzy and concentrated on the lush coral instead. Camille gave an inarticulate shout through her regulator, pointing excitedly ahead. A six-foot green moray eel emerged from a crevice, its sinuous body gracefully undulating in the current. It was both beautiful and slightly frightening, but the eel didn't threaten us as it glided by. We watched in awe as it disappeared back into the coral.

Unable to suppress a grin, I turned to Clay. He squeezed my hand, his eyes crinkling and his touch lingering as we swam on with hands clasped. Every stroke of his thumb made my body hum like a live wire. We'd made love three times, unable to get enough of each other, and had barely made it to the dive boat on time.

Unfortunately, we also had jobs to do. This dive excursion represented the last of our vacation. Clay and Nate were going out to discuss their decision over drinks later, while I would be back to work organizing tomorrow's gala.

The afternoon air was balmy, with a light breeze as we climbed back on board. I could feel Camille's eyes on me, observing my every move as if she were trying to piece together a puzzle.

Clay's intense gaze met mine as we removed our gear. He bent over to whisper in my ear, "You're killing me in that wetsuit now that I know what's underneath."

I laughed and sent him a flirty look back. "That goes double for you. Good thing we still have a couple of nights together, even if it's back to the business portion of the trip."

His fingers brushed against my arm ever so lightly before he turned away to join Nate at the bow of the boat. My skin came alive where he'd touched it.

Camille sidled up next to me, a smile playing at her lips as we started back to the Key. "You two seem awfully close all of a sudden. I like the two of you together."

I ducked my head, a flush heating my face. I'd just met Camille, but I was well aware that she had known Clay her entire life, having grown up next to the Harmons. But her friendly, laidback nature made her easy to talk to.

"It's... well, Clay and I have crossed a line. We're more than boss and assistant now." The words tumbled out in a rush. "I don't know how much more, but things have definitely shifted between us."

Camille's eyes lit up. "I knew it! The air is practically

electric between you two. Clay's never this relaxed around anyone. He's always so driven, you know?" She nodded toward where Clay and Nate were leaning against the railing, their profiles outlined in gold as the sun sank lower in the sky. "Seeing him like this, it's like he's a whole different person. I've known him for ages, and I didn't even realize this side of him existed. It must be because of you."

I followed Camille's gaze, watching as Clay threw back his head and laughed, the sound carrying over the hum of the engine. He turned, as if sensing my eyes on him, and the smile that lit his face was like the sun breaking through clouds on a stormy day. My heart stuttered at the sight. The idea that I could bring out a different side of Clay was exhilarating and a little nerve-wracking. But as I watched him chatting animatedly with Nate, his eyes occasionally flicking back to me, all I felt was an overwhelming sense of happiness. Before I knew it, the motor powered down to idle speed as we entered the canal. Then we were tied up and the experience was over.

"Come on," Clay called to me, his eyes warm as he gathered our beach bags. "We should head back."

"Sure thing," I replied, returning his smile as I followed him off the boat. He draped an arm over my shoulders, and I placed my hand on the small of his back, rubbing slowly.

As we walked back to our cottage, white-and-pink plumeria trees fringed the brick pathway, creating a beautiful atmosphere that matched my euphoric mood. Then we ran into Laurent. His face was a mixture of disdain and boredom as he approached Clay, who asked how he was.

"I'm bored," he complained loudly, making sure everyone around could hear him. "I long for the city. For action and civilization. Though I appreciate your intentions, I cannot wait for the gala tomorrow night so that I can return to France victorious."

Clay and I dropped our arms from each other, and I tried to remain professional despite the anger rising inside me. This man had been nothing but rude and condescending since he'd arrived, and I couldn't stand how he treated everyone like they were beneath him.

"Laurent, I understand you have high standards," Clay said smoothly, stepping up to handle the situation in his usual confident manner. "But I assure you, our team has put together an exceptional event for tomorrow. I believe you'll be pleasantly surprised. And impressed."

"That remains to be seen," Laurent muttered, still unsatisfied. "I have not heard anything further regarding my offer. Surely you cannot be considering that other... woman's bid?"

Clay's face took on a hard edge and Laurent deflated a little. "We are taking Celeste's offer every bit as seriously as yours and still deliberating. We will announce the winner tomorrow morning. The gala is simply a celebration."

Laurent stared between us, his teeth grinding. "Yes, I can see how busy you all are. Most unprofessional, and I am not accustomed to being treated like this. Perhaps I will just withdraw my offer altogether." He turned away from us, stalking off toward his own accommodations.

"Go ahead without me," Clay said, touching my arm gently. His voice still had that edge to it, but now that we were alone, he let his irritation show through. "I'll smooth things over with Laurent and join you shortly."

"All right. Good luck."

I gave him a sympathetic look before entering the cottage alone. The tension in my body started to dissipate as I stepped into the shower, letting the warm water wash away the stress of dealing with Laurent. It was a stark reminder that Clay and I weren't on a lover's tryst.

As I stood there, the steady stream of water cascading down my skin, I went over the plans for the gala in my head, mentally ticking off all the last-minute details that needed to be handled. After my shower, I wrapped myself in a plush towel and stepped out into my bedroom. Just as I finished dressing, I heard the front door open and Clay's footsteps. I entered the living room to find him standing with his arms crossed, his eyes betraying a lingering frustration.

He dropped onto a couch and scrubbed a hand through his hair. Tufts of it stuck up. "Asshole. I'm paying for everything, and all that man ever does is bitch."

"Come here," I said, moving to sit beside him on the couch. "Let me help you relax." Leaning into me, Clay allowed me to rub his rock-hard shoulders. "Did you calm him down?"

He groaned as I rubbed a tight knot, then nodded. "Yeah. He's a prick, but he wants Podium. He knew he pushed me as far as I'll go and backed down, apologizing."

His muscles gradually loosened under my touch, and warmth spread between us. Clay turned his head to look at me, and our eyes locked. Slowly, our lips met.

All three times we'd made love had been different. The first time had been raw power and passion. The second he'd been tender and caring, making sure he was gentle. And the third time had been absolutely perfect—the result of a man who understood what I liked and wanted to give it to me. This kiss was an echo.

Now I knew what he needed. To feel powerful. I closed my fist in his hair, pulling him in as I parted his lips with my tongue. I bit down gently on his lip, making him groan against my mouth. For a long, breathless moment, all the complications and distractions of our world disappeared, leaving only us.

When we finally broke apart, he closed his eyes and rested his forehead against mine. "Thank you," he whispered, pressing a gentle kiss to my forehead. "I needed that."

I decided to inject a little humor into the situation. "Consider it a perk of the job. Though I don't remember seeing it in my contract."

As I'd hoped, his face lit up in a smile as he leaned back. "I'm sure neither of us expected this to happen, but right now, you're exactly what I need."

And hearing that made my heart feel like it was too big for my chest. We were such different people living such different lives. But for the first time, a glimmer of hope alighted within me. Maybe we could make this work.

Chapter Eighteen

Clay

I LEANED back against the couch, a contented sigh escaping my lips. Elise sat beside me, her presence a warmth that lingered even though her fingers had stopped their soothing massage. But her warm side touching mine was a vivid reminder of the kiss we had just shared. The frustration of dealing with Laurent had faded, replaced by a sense of relaxed contentment I hadn't anticipated.

My gaze drifted toward the turquoise ocean shimmering in the distance beyond my pool. The late afternoon sun turned the water into a canvas of shimmering gold and aqua, a breathtaking contrast to the sleek steel and glass of my normal Manhattan world. A warm, inviting world I wanted to immerse myself in.

"Do you want to go for a walk?" I asked, the words escaping before I could stop them. I wasn't one for casual strolls, especially not when a crucial business deal hung in the balance. But the idea of spending time with Elise, away

from the confines of work and negotiations, was unexpect-
edly appealing.

Elise's smile widened. "I'd love to," she replied, her
voice light and happy.

We stepped out of the cottage and onto the beach, the
air soft and fragrant with the scent of salt and seagrass. I
slipped off my loafers, feeling the fine, white sand between
my toes, a novel sensation for a man accustomed to Italian
leather and polished marble floors.

"You mentioned wanting to explore new opportunities
within the company," I said, my gaze on the endless stretch
of turquoise water before us. "What type of position are you
interested in?"

Elise was quiet for a moment, her dark blue eyes
thoughtful. "To be honest, I'm intrigued by GreenDrive.
The electric vehicle industry is fascinating, and I'd love to
be involved somehow."

"It's definitely a game-changer," I agreed, my mind
already racing with the possibilities my new venture might
bring. "We're still in the early stages of the buyout, so there's
plenty of time to explore different options."

"Good, I wouldn't want to rush into anything." She
laughed and the sound was like honey dripping from a
spoon, sweet and rich. "Besides, I've got a feeling you're not
exactly eager to find a new assistant."

"You're damn right about that. You're too good at what
you do. No one's ever lasted this long."

"That's because you terrorized all the others into quit-
ting," she teased, her smile lighting up her face.

I stopped walking and turned to face her, taking her
hand in mine. "No," I said, my voice softening as our fingers
intertwined. "That's because you have steel inside you,

Elise. You've done excellent work the past three years and I'm sorry I haven't told you that more often."

"It's all right," she said as we began strolling again, heading toward the waterline. "It's not your nature. You expressed your appreciation in more... subtle ways."

I was pretty sure she just called me an asshole in very polite language, but I let the subject drop. Her hand was soft and warm within mine, and I enjoyed brushing my thumb over the back of it.

"Tell me about your family, how you grew up in Pennsylvania," I said.

She turned her gaze to the distant horizon, hesitating. "Millbrook is a small town. Nothing special." Her voice was soft, almost distant, as if she were revisiting a world far removed from the luxury surrounding us. Something in her tone, a guarded note I hadn't heard before, sparked my curiosity.

"Tell me more," I urged, squeezing her hand gently.

With a line between her brows, she began to speak. Snippets of a childhood filled with more responsibility than carefree days emerged—a family struggling to make ends meet, a loving but often absent father who chased one get rich quick scheme after another, a mother who worked tirelessly as a seamstress to provide for them. She talked about missing school events and activities, about yearning for things she couldn't have.

"I learned to depend on myself," she said quietly, her gaze still fixed on the distant horizon. "I had to. There were no fairy godmothers in Millbrook."

"So you don't believe in fairy tales?" I asked, a teasing lilt in my voice.

Her gaze snapped to mine, her dark blue eyes intense. "No," she said, her voice firm. "I don't."

I studied her face, her expression a mix of defiance and something else I couldn't quite decipher. "I get the feeling there's more to the story," I said, my curiosity piqued.

Elise was quiet for a long moment, the only sound the gentle rhythm of the waves lapping against the shore. Then she took a deep breath and began to tell me about a resin angel she'd brought on the trip. A memento she'd carried with her for years, though it was anything but a happy memory. She recounted the story of her father's broken promise, of the bowling ball that arrived instead of the crystal cat, of her mother's quiet strength, and the gift of the angel.

"It's a reminder to make my own dreams come true," she said, her voice softening. "And not wait around for happy endings to be handed to me."

I processed her story as we reached the end of the beach and the kayak kiosk. As we turned around and headed back, the gentle rhythm of the waves formed a soothing backdrop to her words. I was struck by her strength, by her determination to forge her own path. I pictured her as a young girl in that small Pennsylvania town, dreaming of a life beyond its borders. A life she'd created for herself, through sheer grit and hard work.

A fierce protectiveness surged through me, a desire to shield her from the disappointments, the hardships she'd faced, all while acknowledging her raw ability and desire to succeed. I found myself wanting to give her everything she'd ever wanted, to smooth her path, to see her dreams realized. I wanted to be the one to show her that happy endings weren't just for fairy tales. That maybe... they could exist in the real world too.

The intensity of these foreign emotions—protective, possessive, even tender—alarmed me.

What the hell is happening to me?

I needed to regain control, to reassert the boundaries I'd carefully erected around myself. "You've done remarkably well," I said, pleased with how steady my voice sounded. "You've built a successful life for yourself, and I admire you for it."

Her hand was still nestled in mine, her fingers delicate yet strong. Despite my attempt to distance myself, I couldn't resist the urge to reassure her, to soothe the sadness that lingered in her eyes. My thumb gently stroked her knuckles, a gesture that surprised me as much as it probably did her.

A grateful smile touched her lips. "Thank you. But I'm no Cinderella. My fairy tale involves a killer resume, not a glass slipper."

Her gentle humor eased the tension that had coiled in my chest. I found myself smiling back, and maybe those self-imposed walls of mine were cracking a little with every shared word, every stolen glance, every touch.

"I'm sorry you had it so rough," I said, my voice soft. "My own childhood was... a very different story."

Elise tilted her head, her expression curious. "Different how?"

"My parents weren't wealthy," I explained, "But they were supportive. My family home was warm and welcoming, and we were comfortably well-off. They encouraged my ambitions, even when those ambitions meant missing family dinners or spending weekends buried in textbooks. They understood my drive, my need to achieve."

"Lucky you," Elise said, her voice light. "I think my mom was terrified by how driven I was. Like it was something unnatural. She wanted me to find a nice, stable job close to home and settle down."

"They even converted our basement into a home office for me when I was fifteen," I continued, a smile touching my lips at the memory. "It wasn't much, but it was my sanctuary, my space to create, to strategize, to dream."

"A teenage boy's dream come true," Elise teased. "Unlimited computer access, no annoying siblings barging in to bug you…"

"Exactly," I said, laughing at the thought of Nate invading my carefully ordered space. Even then, I'd thrived on structure and solitude, qualities my parents seemed to recognize instinctively.

"And you just channeled all that energy into building your empire," she said, her voice tinged with a trace of awe. "It's an amazing accomplishment."

Elise's simple compliment filled me with satisfaction, more than any award or bank balance. "Harvard changed everything. That's where I really came into my own, surrounded by people who were just as driven, just as ambitious, as I was. That's where I developed the confidence to believe I could achieve anything. To take risks."

She remained silent but squeezed my hand as a warm wave splashed over our feet.

"I started my first company while I was there," I continued, the gentle breeze ruffling through my hair. "It was a software company, a new approach to data analysis, and it took off like a rocket. Three years later, I sold it for a ridiculous amount of money. I haven't looked back since."

"No, you certainly haven't. And I understand what you mean about moving from home changing things," she said, nodding. "Going away to college was my escape from Millbrook."

"It was a lucky thing for me that you did." And worried

my words made light of her very serious story, I bent down to brush a soft kiss over her lips.

We continued our walk, and the sun was beginning to dip lower in the sky, painting the clouds with hues of gold and crimson. I felt a sense of peace I hadn't experienced in years, a lightness I attributed to the break from the usual pressures of my life.

Except the break was over.

As we walked along the row of cottages, reality reasserted itself. My thoughts drifted to Laurent, to Celeste, to the vast differences in their personalities and their approaches to business. I admired Laurent's ruthless ambition, his vast global empire, his relentless pursuit of success. That drive, that hunger for more... it mirrored my own. He was the logical choice, the one who would maximize profits and expand Podium's reach. And give the current staff very sizeable bonuses.

But Celeste's warmth, her genuine compassion for Podium's employees, and her heartfelt commitment to the company's legacy tugged at something deeper within me. I thought about Nate's words, urging me to find a different path, to think beyond the bottom line. I glanced at Elise beside me, her hand warm and reassuring in mine. I was surprised at how her simple honesty, her unwavering determination to build her own life, had shifted my perspective. Had I been too focused on the numbers, on the relentless pursuit of more, and forgotten about the human element?

My mind was in turmoil, a battleground of ambition and... something else I couldn't dare acknowledge.

Finally, I let go of Elise's hand as we stepped off the sand and onto the cool grass. We slipped our shoes back on, and I held the door open for her, my fingers brushing lightly against hers as we entered the cottage. The air inside was cool and fragrant, a welcome contrast to the humid air outside.

"I need to go freshen up before I meet Nate," I said, trying to ignore the disappointment that shadowed my words. I wanted to linger. I wanted to stay with her.

"Of course," she said, her voice soft. "I'll see you later."

But as she turned to head to her room, something snapped inside me. I reached for her, pulling her against me. Her eyes widened in surprise, and her breath hitched. The warmth of her body against mine sent a heady jolt of desire through me.

"I promised Nate I'd go with him to a local brewpub on the next island. Kind of a brother thing."

Her mouth was inches from mine. "You don't owe me an explanation. I'll have dinner at the bar. It's fine."

Except it wasn't fine. I didn't understand the push and pull inside me, the roaring urge to tell Nate to go to hell and stay right here. I kissed her, unable to resist the need to taste her lips, to feel her body pressed against mine.

Then my phone buzzed with a text. I broke away with a reluctant laugh. "Two guesses who that is." I pulled out my phone and confirmed it was Nate asking if I was ready.

Her smile had a sly curve to it. "Go have your brother time. Maybe we can pick up where we left off when you get back."

I growled and pulled her tight again. "I like the sound of that. I'll be back soon."

But as I made my way to meet Nate, a nagging voice in the back of my mind whispered that this was too good to be true. I'd learned long ago that in business and in life, if something seemed too perfect, it usually was. I pushed the thought aside, determined to enjoy the evening. Because that was the other thing I'd learned since arriving on Calypso Key—don't analyze every second, and just live in the moment.

And right now I was having one hell of a good moment.

Chapter Nineteen

Elise

THE SILENCE that settled over the cottage after Clay left was heavier than I expected. Heavier and more... intimate. I wandered toward the pool, then just as quickly turned around. A wave of heat washed over me, the memory of Clay's kisses, his touch, his words... still tingling on my skin. A swim wasn't going to cut it—that only brought thoughts of our first kiss. What I needed was a distraction, and a long, hot soak sounded like the perfect antidote.

The bathroom beckoned, a sanctuary of marble and chrome. I filled the smooth white marble tub, adding a generous amount of lavender-scented bath salts. As I sank into the warm water, the fragrance enveloped me, soothing my muscles.

This trip had been incredible. From the thrilling dive, to the unexpected kayaking adventure, to Clay and I becoming... whatever we were. It was more than I had ever dared to dream of. I'd finally seen the man behind the CEO façade, the man who could laugh and relax, the man who had opened his heart to *me*.

I closed my eyes, willing my mind to quiet, but a familiar voice whispered in the back of my mind. It was a voice I'd learned to trust, the voice of hard-won experience: *If something seems too good to be true, it probably is.* And Clay Harmon falling for me definitely fell into that category.

What could I possibly offer a man like Clay? I was just an assistant, a cog in the vast machine of his corporation. The disparity between us yawned like a chasm, and I felt myself teetering on the edge.

With a frustrated sigh, I sat up, water cascading off my shoulders. This bath, intended to soothe my troubled mind, had only intensified my anxieties. As I stepped out of the tub, my reflection caught my eye. The woman in the mirror looked lost, vulnerable—everything I had promised myself I would never be again. Clenching my jaw, I was determined not to let my fears consume me. I would face this head-on, just like every other challenge in my life.

"I need a drink. Preferably an alcoholic one."

Perhaps a change of scenery and a glass of wine would help clear my head, give me some perspective on my whirlwind romance with Clay. As I approached, the vibrant atmosphere washed over me. The bar pulsed with life—vacationers letting loose and several locals enjoying the music. A lively band on the small stage filled the room with irresistible tropical rhythms.

Making my way to the bar, I caught the bartender's eye. "Chardonnay, please," I said, raising my voice just enough to be heard over the music. He returned moments later with a glass of golden liquid that sparkled invitingly in the warm lighting.

As I sipped the rich wine, I let my gaze wander around the room. The joyous energy was infectious, and my worry about Clay eased from my mind. My eyes settled on a corner table, and I blinked in surprise. Camille sat deep in conversation with Monica, the yoga instructor.

I hadn't realized they knew each other. They were clearly having a great time, heads close together, punctuating their conversation with bursts of laughter. For a moment, I considered joining them, but they looked so engrossed in their chat that I decided not to interrupt.

Instead, I turned my attention to the band. The lead singer's voice was sultry and smooth, weaving through the instrumental beats like silk. My foot tapped along to the rhythm, and a smile tugged at the corners of my mouth.

I took another sip of wine, savoring the flavors as they danced across my tongue. The rich, heady notes seemed to harmonize with the music, creating a perfect sensory melody. I closed my eyes for a moment, letting the lively atmosphere envelop me.

The band had just finished a particularly lively number when I felt a presence at my elbow. The hairs on the back of my neck stood up before I even turned to look.

"Well, well. If it isn't Clay Harmon's little... assistant."

I knew that voice. Smooth as silk and twice as slippery. Laurent DuBois.

I turned slowly, steeling myself. His cream colored linen suit was pressed and impeccable, his hair artfully slicked back, and he held a snifter of cognac in one manicured hand. His lips were curved in what I suppose he thought was a charming smile, but to me, it looked more like a predator baring its teeth.

"Good evening, Mr. DuBois," I said, proud of how

steady my voice sounded, and hoping the formal address would send him on his way.

He tsked, wagging a finger. "Come now, we're all friends now. Call me Laurent." He leaned in, his expensive cologne drifting over me. "I must say, I'm surprised to see you here alone. Trouble in paradise already?"

"I have no idea what you mean."

"Only that I never expected you to let Clay out of your clutches." He arched a brow. "When I saw you two earlier, I noticed he had his arm around you, and naturally assumed the mighty billionaire found someone new to play with."

My heart stuttered to a stop. "Excuse me?"

His eyes glittered with something I couldn't quite name. Malice? Amusement? "I wonder, my dear, if you truly understand the... nature of your relationship with our dear Clay."

My grip tightened on my glass. "I don't see how any of this is your concern."

Laurent chuckled, the sound grating on my nerves. "Oh, come now. Surely you don't think... No, you're a smart girl. You must know that men like Clay Harmon don't fall for little nobodies." He waved his hand dismissively. "You're a distraction, nothing more. A pretty little toy to pass the time."

His words hit me like a physical blow, voicing every insecurity I'd been battling. Reinforcing every statement my inner voice had been screaming at me. I opened my mouth to respond, but he continued, his tone dripping with false sympathy.

"Don't take it personally, *chérie*. It is simply the way of things. When this deal is done, he'll move on to the next shiny object that catches his eye. Best to enjoy it while it lasts, *non*?"

I wanted to argue, to defend myself and Clay. But Laurent's words had found purchase in the cracks of my confidence, widening them into chasms of doubt. I sat there, speechless and my mouth agape, as he raised his glass in a mocking toast.

"To fleeting fancies," he said with a wink, before sauntering away and leaving me alone with the bitter taste of insecurity on my tongue.

The music continued to play, the crowd continued to laugh and dance, but suddenly, I felt completely and utterly alone.

I stared into my half-empty wine glass, Laurent's words echoing in my mind. The bar's cheerful atmosphere now felt like mockery. I was considering jumping in the ocean fully clothed when a gentle hand touched my arm.

"Elise? Are you okay?"

I glanced up at Camille, her face etched with concern. I tried to smile, but it felt more like a grimace.

"I'm fine," I lied, my voice coming out in a waver.

Camille's eyes narrowed. "Bullshit," she said flatly. "Nate pointed that guy out to me—the Frenchman. Said to watch out for him. And from what Monica and I just saw, he looked about as charming as a shark with a toothache."

A surprised laugh escaped me at her description, breaking through the fog of my distress.

"Come on," Camille said, tugging gently at my arm. "Monica and I have a table. Join us."

Part of me wanted to decline, to retreat and lick my wounds in private. But Camille's warmth was like a lifeline, and I found myself following her to the corner table.

Monica greeted me with both a smile and a creased brow, but her calm presence still eased my frazzled nerves.

Camille signaled a waiter, ordering a round of drinks I didn't catch the name of.

"So," Camille said once we were settled, "What did that creep say to you?"

I hesitated, then the words tumbled out. All of them. Every disgusting, terrifying thing he'd said

Camille's eyes flashed with anger. "That slimy, arrogant..." She took a long, cleansing breath. "Elise, honey, don't listen to him. That guy wouldn't recognize genuine attraction if it slapped him across that smug, French face of his."

My heart hardened, and I could imagine armor plating encircling it as I shook my head. "I learned to keep my head firmly on my shoulders growing up. In just a few days, I seem to have completely abandoned that. Laurent might be a Grade-A asshole, but I can't deny what he said makes sense. Clay could have anyone. Why would he choose me?"

Monica leaned forward, her voice soft but firm. "You understand him, don't you? Camille was just telling me that you're the only assistant who hasn't quit—he sounds like he appreciates a strong woman."

Camille nodded emphatically. "Exactly. I've known Clay for years, and he's different this trip. Nate keeps remarking on it."

Their words were comforting but doubt still gnawed at me. "I just... I don't know if I can trust this. It all seems too good to be true."

Camille's expression softened. "I know the feeling. Love often does." She took a drink of the Calypso Breeze. "And my farfetched romance with Nate worked out, didn't it?"

I shook my head, refusing to be soothed. "But Nate's a very different kind of man than Clay, isn't he?"

Camille hesitated, then sighed. "You're right, they're

very different. Nate was a notorious playboy before he met me, but that was never him. It was more of a cry for help—he just wanted someone to accept him."

"Clay just assumes the world does what he wants!" I hissed, trying not to raise my voice. "I don't think he even knows the word unsure."

Monica cocked her head. "Are you sure about that? Maybe he's afraid to let anyone get too close. We all talk about how incredible it would be to be extremely wealthy, but I'm sure it comes with its fair share of problems too."

I sighed. I'd known Clay for three years, and what I'd glimpsed in the last few days contrasted drastically with the man I'd come to know. But which was the real Clay Harmon? "Guys, it's not just a broken heart we're discussing here. I could be jeopardizing my entire career."

Camille's supportive smile vanished. "That is definitely something I never had to worry about. And it's an extremely valid point."

I inhaled a lungful of air and placed my hands flat on the table. "I'm taking an insane risk here. He's not. We were even discussing promotions for me—because I've earned it, not because I'm his... whatever. If I walk this back now, I can probably salvage everything. But if I just give in to my heart and let things work out, I could lose it all."

Monica reached over and patted my hand. "Or gain everything you've ever dreamed of. But only you can decide that. I've seen more budding romances here than I can count. Some flourish, some wither. But the ones meant to be? They find a way, against all odds. Trust your heart, Elise. It knows the truth, even when your mind doubts."

I slid my chair back and stood. "Thanks, you two. You rescued me at just the right moment, but I think I'll head back now." I met Camille's eyes. "I really like seeing you and Nate together. It's obvious you're perfect for each other. But the situation with Clay and me is so, so different. This is real life, Camille. I'm not Cinderella, and there's no glass slippers in sight."

As I WALKED with wooden steps, the path back to the cottage stretched before me. Each step was heavy with trepidation as Laurent's taunts ricocheted off the inside of my skull.

A pretty little toy. A fleeting fancy.

As much as I wanted to dismiss his words, they echoed my own fears. I couldn't deny the growing feelings I had for Clay, but I was also terrified he didn't share them. We had a connection—that was undeniable. But there was a giant, yawning gulf between connection and love.

I felt so stupid.

How could I have allowed myself to become involved with him, risking my career in the process? And worse, it was much more than physical. I'd fallen for him—in just a few days! Then I stopped in my tracks and exhaled a deep, long, miserable sigh.

"Time to be honest with yourself. Own up to it." I trudged on, my steps leaden.

I'd been half in love with Clay Harmon for years, despite his cool aloofness at work. Despite his icy reserve. Hell, that was half the attraction—he was so unattainable! Therefore, it was completely safe to worship him from afar.

Here in this heady, sultry tropical paradise with him, it hadn't taken much to tip my poor heart over the edge.

I paused at the cottage door, my hand hovering over the knob. Clay's cottage, not mine. I was merely a guest. For the first time in my life, I wanted to believe the fairy tale! I wanted Prince Charming to sweep me away. Was I making a mistake in deciding to pull back from the precipice?

After opening the door, I entered and crossed the floor into my bedroom. My eye fell on the angel on my dresser. After shutting the door, I marched over and picked it up—maybe this figurine I'd carried around for years would help guide me. It was warm in my hand, familiar. A very hard lesson I'd learned at an early age. Was I in the process of learning another one? But Clay and I were so good together! More similar than I'd ever imagined.

As I transferred the angel to my other hand, it slipped.

I gasped as it hit the marble floor and cracked into half a dozen pieces. Broken.

A sob escaped me as I stared down at the empty promise. The reminder that I couldn't afford to believe in tall tales. The sweet angel who had one final lesson to teach me. With tears sliding down my face, I raised my eyes to the shut door.

Beyond that threshold lay a conversation I dreaded. One that would shatter the fragile dream I'd allowed myself to embrace, if only for a brief, perfect moment. With a long sigh, I prepared for bed. Come tomorrow, I'd be ready to confront the fairy tale before it shattered me to pieces.

Chapter Twenty

Clay

THE CONCH REPUBLIC, a remodeled cannery on a bluff, exuded a warm, homey atmosphere with its exposed ductwork, metal roof, and abundance of wood. Situated on Dove Key, Calypso Key's larger neighbor to the north, the brewpub faced east with expansive ocean views. Nate and I sat in a corner booth, the clinking of glasses and low hum of conversation around us providing a comfortable backdrop.

We'd come there to discuss the sale and gala, but business was damn near the last thing on my mind. I'd hardly processed a word we'd said over dinner, and his current point about Celeste and her father creating a thriving family business went in one ear and out the other. The entire day ran through my head—the kayaking, followed by the incredible morning in bed, then diving with Elise in the afternoon.

"Clay!" Nate almost shouted, bringing me back to earth.

I jumped. "Sorry. What were you saying?"

He just stared at me. "What the hell? Is this about Elise?"

"Is what about Elise?"

He smiled, then his lips spread into a huge grin until his shoulders shook. "Uh, the fact that we're hours from sealing the biggest deal of your career and your mind is miles away. Something sure happened between you two. Spill, brother."

My first thought was to evade—my natural reaction to put someone on the defensive. But this was Nate, and I realized I wanted to talk about it. Maybe even needed to talk about it. "*We* happened. Elise and me. We slept together for the first time this morning." A laugh tumbled out of my mouth and I took a long drink of beer. "And the second and third."

His amused expression remained, but his eyes turned evaluative. "I thought you two were awfully chummy on the boat. Obviously, you took my advice. That was quick."

"I know." I scrubbed a hand over the stubble on my jaw. "It's new. All of it. And she's my assistant, for God's sake."

Nate studied me for a long moment. "All valid points, as I said before. I hear a but coming."

I looked away, sweeping my eyes over the exposed brick walls of the brewery. When I glanced back at Nate, I knew my expression had given me away. "But she knows me better than any other woman I've dated. I never let any of them get close to me. Elise is very different."

"She's had to know you well—that's her job. Are you serious about her?" Nate studied my face, his own neutral and giving no hint of his feelings.

I hesitated, not knowing how to answer. There was no denying the attraction, the chemistry between us. I finally replied, "I'm her boss and that makes her off-limits. But at the same time, yeah, I want to see where this goes."

My thoughts drifted to my past relationships, and I shook my head. "Every woman I've dated wanted something from me, whether it was my money, status, or connections. Not a single damn one cared about me. As a man. As a human being. But this feels different. Maybe because Elise works for me, so she's naturally seen me at my best and worst. I let my guard down around her, especially since we came down here."

Nate smirked, taking another swig of his drink. "You might be in love with her, you know."

I swear I broke out in a cold sweat. "Love? No way." But deep down, part of me whispered that maybe I *could* fall in love with her. In time. I wasn't ready to listen to that inner voice.

"Hey, being in love isn't the worst thing in the world. Camille definitely straightened me out, didn't she?" Nate grinned and saluted me with his beer. "As ordered."

Grateful for the change in tone, I laughed and we clinked glasses. "Yeah, but both of you got a little more than you bargained for out of the situation."

Mischief flickered in Nate's eyes. "No complaints here. And I've got some surprises up my sleeve."

"Oh?" I raised a brow, curious. "Like what?"

"Like none of your damn beeswax," Nate replied with a laugh.

"Fine, keep your secrets," I retorted, smiling and taking another drink of my beer. Nate's obvious happiness was enough for me. An errant thought ran through my head.

Could I find the same happiness with Elise?

I pushed it away, ready to discuss the subject we were there for. "Let's talk about the sale. What's your take on Laurent and Celeste?"

Nate leaned back in the booth, crossing his arms. "I had another meeting with both of them today while you were frolicking in bed." He ignored my scowl and continued with a grin, "Told them I was done being the spokesperson for Podium. My focus will be squarely on the new venture Camille and I are working on. Both were okay with that. Laurent acted like he couldn't care less."

"Who do you think we should go with for the sale?" I asked.

Nate snorted, clearly having formed an opinion. "How about anyone but that puffed-up French asshole?"

I laughed, but it fell into a sigh. "Yeah, I had to smooth things over with Laurent earlier. He threatened to pull his offer."

"Seriously?" Nate asked, taken aback. Then he became pensive. "His bid is mighty tempting, but is money the most important thing? What about all the people who work for Podium? You know, our employees?"

I nodded. "I know. We need to consider more than just the highest bidder but let me point out that those employees will benefit directly from a more lucrative sale amount in the form of higher bonuses. Let's sleep on it and make the final decision in the morning."

"Sleep?" Nate grinned. "Something tells me you won't be getting much rest tonight."

I smiled back, already itching to return to the resort. And Elise. "Yeah, probably not."

After Nate and I parted upon returning to Calypso Key, I made my way back to the cottage. My anticipation built with every step. What would she be wearing? Maybe something black and sexy? Maybe nothing at all? I couldn't wait to find out.

As I opened the door, I found Elise sitting on the couch, dressed in leggings and an oversized shirt. As soon as she saw me, she slowly rose to her feet, her posture stiff and aloof.

"Hey," I said cautiously, sensing that something was off.

"Hi." Her voice was quiet and pensive.

"Is everything all right?" I tried to read her expression. Her eyes were red and puffy, further raising alarm bells.

"I've been thinking this evening." Elise hesitated for a moment before opening her mouth. "There's no easy way to say this. We need to stop what we're doing. Our relationship or whatever you want to call it... it's a mistake."

"Wait, what?" I stammered, a cold hollowness forming in my stomach. "Why? What happened?"

"We need to focus on the sale and the gala. Why we're here, Clay. Our personal lives shouldn't interfere with our work." She dropped her eyes to the floor.

"Elise, we can handle both," I said, trying to ignore the way my heart pounded in my chest. The way her words were causing something like panic to knot my insides. "This doesn't have to be an either-or situation."

"Please," she pleaded, still refusing to meet my gaze. "I need to concentrate on what's important right now."

"And obviously that's not me. Or us," I barked, the panic morphing to hurt. Rejection rose within me like bile.

"Clay, you've worked so hard for this! And so have I. Neither of us can afford to be distracted right now." The woman who had been so open and passionate toward me just hours ago now stood like a stranger. "Don't get upset. I need some space, all right?"

"Oh, I see." My heart pounded in my ears, heat flaming across my face. "You need. Why doesn't anyone ever give a shit about what I might need? Or am I only here to grant your every wish? Is that it?"

Finally, she snapped her eyes up to meet mine, a gasp escaping. "Of course not! I haven't asked you for anything."

"Except a promotion. Or did you think you already got that?" I was a volcano beginning to erupt, a smoky, red haze forming before my eyes. "Tell me what's going on, dammit! You've done a complete one-eighty since I left a couple of hours ago. Why?"

Elise shook her head, her jaw set tight. "I just had a moment to think about all that's happened. And when I pulled out the schedule for tomorrow, I realized we've gotten completely off track here. I'm your assistant, Clay. Nothing more."

I inhaled sharply, her words knifing through me. We stood six feet apart, staring at each other. I didn't know how to respond—I wasn't used to being in this position. Hell, I went through life doing everything possible not to feel like this.

Lost. Hurt.

And worst of all—vulnerable.

So, without another word, I whirled around and marched to my bedroom. The door made a satisfying crash as I slammed it behind me.

Frustration and confusion swirled within me as I paced my bedroom, trying to make sense of her sudden change in attitude. The woman who had shared her warmth, laughter, and body with me had disappeared, replaced by this cold and distant professional. My hands balled into fists.

"Shit," I muttered under my breath, raking my fingers through my hair. I thought of my words to Nate—about my prior relationships. I had allowed myself to believe that what we shared was real, that Elise was different from all the other women.

I was a fool.

Early in the trip, she'd said it out loud—that she wanted a job with more responsibility. Elise didn't want me, she wanted what I could give her. Just like all the others. It had nothing to do with me as a man.

The vulnerability faded away, replaced by a cold, icy anger that was much more familiar. Much more understandable. This pull-back from Elise was a trick to gain control and get me to do her bidding.

That would never happen.

But she was right about one thing. Tomorrow was the day I had been working toward for years. The sale of Podium. I needed to concentrate on making the best decision for the company Nate and I had built together. Not lament a lost relationship that had never even gotten off the ground.

Sitting down on the edge of the bed, I considered both Laurent and Celeste as potential buyers. While Laurent was an arrogant prick, his experience with sports teams could lead Podium to even greater success. Not to mention he'd made an offer that was damn hard to ignore. Celeste, on the other hand, had a genuine passion for the opportunity and cared about the people working for Podium. But was that enough?

As much as I tried to avoid it, my thoughts kept drifting back to Elise. I undressed and climbed into bed, trying not to think about the fact that she had been right here mere hours ago. The sheets still smelled of her, the pillow too. I still longed for her—to be inside her, to talk to her, to hold her in my arms and stroke her soft, creamy skin.

With a snarl, I punched the pillow and settled into it. I

pushed her out of my mind to focus on what truly mattered: the future of Podium.

"Tomorrow," I murmured to myself with determination. "Everything will become clear." And forcing my clenched muscles to relax, I cleared my mind to sleep, preparing for the life-changing decision that awaited me.

Chapter Twenty-One

Clay

I BLINKED my eyes open to dim light coming into my bedroom. After rubbing the sleep from them, I tried to shake off the lingering remnants of dreams. All night, I'd been consumed with thoughts of Elise, her guarded face from last night etched into my memory. Overnight, my anger had dulled to a quiet, hollow despondency. I wanted to go to her but held back. This self-doubt was unfamiliar territory for me.

And I didn't like it one damn bit.

I swung my legs over the side of the bed, running a hand over the stubble on my jaw. A quick glance at the clock told me it was almost seven. I changed into slacks and a polo shirt and shaved, but my eyes were still bloodshot. With a sigh, I made my way into the living room and dialed room service, ordering a continental breakfast and fresh coffee. Enough for two. Even though I had a breakfast meeting with Nate soon, eating now might help settle my stomach as well as my mind.

As I waited, I tried to focus on the reports on my laptop screen. Except the words blurred together, meaningless. Instead, my thoughts drifted back to Elise and how different she'd been last night.

Why?

What had caused that sudden change?

A young man from room service arrived quickly, setting up breakfast on the cottage's dining table before bowing out. I poured a cup of coffee, the rich scent not soothing me as I sat down. My restless, confused night had convinced me of one thing—Elise's attitude shift hadn't happened in a vacuum. Something had caused it. I was hurt and pissed off last night, not able to think clearly. And I'd lashed out at her because of it. But I wasn't going to let things drop between us.

We were too good together, dammit.

The sound of a door creaking open pulled me from my musings. I glanced up as Elise shuffled out of her room, her hair disheveled and dark circles under her eyes. She looked haggard, like she hadn't slept at all.

"Morning," I said softly, my stomach twisting. "I ordered some breakfast. And coffee."

"Thanks," she murmured, offering me a shaky smile.

Taking the hint, I poured her a cup of coffee and gestured to the seat opposite me. "Please, sit down," I urged, trying to keep my voice gentle.

She hesitated, then sank into the chair next to me, wrapping her hands around the warm mug.

I inhaled, steeling myself. "I want to apologize for yelling last night. You caught me really off guard, and I didn't handle it well. I'm sorry."

"Thank you," she murmured back, her eyes flicking briefly to meet mine before darting away again.

"Can I ask you something?" I ventured cautiously. "*Why* did you change your mind? Did something specific happen?"

At first, Elise didn't respond, taking a slow sip of her coffee as if gathering her thoughts. Finally, she looked up at me, her gaze filled with uncertainty and vulnerability. I held my breath, waiting for her answer.

"Clay, I... Ever since sparks started to fly between us, I've had doubts. A billionaire falling for his assistant? It just seems so... unrealistic. A childish dream, and I told you I don't believe in those. You've dated supermodels and movie stars, for God's sake!"

Anger flared in me at that, but I remained quiet, letting her talk. She paused, taking a deep breath before continuing. "Last night at the bar, I ran into Laurent. He basically said the same thing, that it was stupid to think someone like you could be serious about me. And it got me thinking... maybe he's right."

Hearing that Laurent was the cause of all this made my blood boil, but I forced myself to stay calm. He wasn't the problem here. I clenched my jaw and focused on what she was saying.

"So I could never fall for a woman who isn't a model?" I asked, the hurt roaring back that she didn't see me as a person capable of genuine feelings. "Do you really think I'm that shallow? That I can't see past someone's surface?"

"That's not it," she tried to explain, her eyes pleading with me to understand. "It's not about you being shallow, it's about... the power dynamics, the expectations, everything that comes with being involved with someone like you. The sneers that you'd be with me when you could have anyone."

But now I was too hurt and pissed off to truly hear her.

Basically, right back to where I was last night. Her words felt like a knife twisting in my chest, and I couldn't shake it. "I promise you, I am not that guy," I said firmly. "I care about you, and what we've started here is real. But if you can't see that—if you'd rather believe that French prick's opinion, then…" I trailed off, not able to finish the thought.

She opened her mouth, but I checked my watch and stood, cutting her off. Things felt worse between us, not better. And I had business to attend to. "I've got to meet Nate about the Podium sale. We're making the final decision." I paused to gather my thoughts. This meeting was something Elise would normally be right next to me at. But not now. "Stay here and work on the gala arrangements."

I stalked from the cottage toward Dorado, an imaginary black cloud looming over my head. Nate and Camille sat at an isolated table. Irritation flashed through me at her presence, along with a hot, sharp pang of jealousy at their closeness. Then I reminded myself that Camille wasn't just Nate's girlfriend, she was his business partner now. She had a right to be here. As I sat down, the weight of Elise's words still felt like an iron anvil in my chest.

Nate noticed immediately that something was wrong. "Hey, what's up with you? You look like shit. That's not the happy *I didn't get any sleep* look I was expecting."

"It's not. Last night didn't go as I expected at all." My words came out clipped and cool, as if I was leading a meeting. And that realization made all the starch dissolve from my spine. I sighed and told them about Elise's change of heart. "She thinks I'm shallow, and that I could never be interested in someone like her. I can't believe I was so wrong about her."

Camille looked thoughtful, then raised her eyes to me. "Don't kill me for what I'm about to say, okay? I think you might be misunderstanding her point of view here. Did she call you shallow?"

"No, but what else would you call it?"

She just stared at me. "Can you really blame her for feeling that way?"

"Blame her?" I snapped, incredulous. "Why should she get to decide who I am? To choose whether I'm capable of caring about someone?"

"She doesn't," Camille said gently. "Look, I ran into her yesterday evening after Laurent said some harsh things to her. I don't think it's about deciding who you are. I don't know Elise well, but she seems very hard-working and independent. She cares about her career and doesn't want to appear like she's after your money. Or your power and influence. She's not one of your arm-candy girls looking for a free ride. Being with you is a huge risk for her, and she's scared of losing everything she's worked so hard for if things don't work out between you two."

I stared right back at Camille, willing that icy rage to rise again. To tell her how wrong she was and that I was the aggrieved party here. Instead, I thumped back in the booth, as numbness washed over me. Because her words struck a chord in me. That was precisely what Elise had said, but I hadn't thought about it from that perspective. I'd been so focused on how hurt I was that I hadn't considered the very real fear Elise must be feeling.

"Shit, I've been an asshole again." I rubbed my eyes, then sat up straight and faced the duo across the table. "I couldn't care less that she's my assistant, or that she doesn't have money like I do. You and I didn't grow up rich, Nate. You know what those relationships with models and actresses got me? Nothing. I felt alone. But the last few days... I've had *fun* with Elise. We've laughed together. Do you have any idea how long it's been since a woman made me laugh?"

Nate stared at me, all traces of his usual humor gone. "Yeah. I do, Clay."

Camille leaned forward, tapping the table to emphasize her point. "What I'm trying to say is that *you're missing the point*. Elise doesn't need to reassure you of her sincerity. You need to reassure her."

I thought back to our two recent painful conversations. I'd said nothing to comfort her. I'd just assumed she wanted to be with me and then got pissed off when she said otherwise. I groaned and wanted to fling my hands in the air. "Look, I'm hell on wheels in the boardroom, but this relationship crap isn't exactly my strong suit. Where do I even begin?"

Camille laughed and shook her head. "By telling her how she makes you feel, you big lug. What you just said about her making you laugh would be a very good start."

"Did her interaction with Laurent last night cause all this?" Nate asked, one hand curled around his coffee mug.

"Yes," I snarled, clenching my fists under the table. "He convinced her that she was nothing but a meaningless fling for me."

Camille frowned, her delicate eyebrows knitting together. "And you didn't make it loud and clear that that wasn't true?"

I sighed, feeling a mix of frustration and embarrassment. "I tried, but I screwed it up. Laurent apparently just reinforced her own fears. I have no idea why he stuck his ugly nose into our private business."

Nate nodded, his gaze steady. "I can tell you why. Because he's a colossal asshole and nothing but trouble.

Which begs the question—why the hell are we considering selling our company to him?"

My eyes locked together with Nate's, and the moment stretched out. Communication passed between us silently, something we'd done since we were kids. Our thoughts synchronized, like two perfectly aligned gears in a well-oiled machine. At the same time, we broke into grim smiles.

"We on the same page, then?" I asked quietly.

Nate's lips curled into a sly, satisfied grin. "Oh, hell yes!"

Camille leaned back in her chair, studying our expressions. Her intuition picked up on the shift in the atmosphere, and she laughed. "Looks like the decision has been made!"

I rose to my feet. "What are we waiting for? Let's go deliver the news in person."

Nate joined me. "Absolutely. I'm ready to crash that bastard against the boards."

"Go get him, guys," Camille added, sipping her coffee as Nate and I marched out of the restaurant.

As the two of us approached Laurent's cottage, my blood thrummed through my body. Anger and determination strengthened every step I took. The lush greenery surrounding the bungalow did nothing to soften my resolve.

"I assume you want to take the lead on this?" Nate asked, his voice low but firm.

"Please. I can't wait."

After we climbed onto the front deck, I knocked on the door. Moments later, it swung open to reveal Laurent, already dressed in a dark-gray suit. As he showed us into his cottage, his expression was one of smug anticipation. I frowned in distaste as his mistress Irina covered her naked body with a silk robe and disappeared into the bathroom.

"*Bonjour*, gentlemen," Laurent said with a smile as he gestured at a bottle of champagne sitting in an ice bucket. "Are you here to congratulate me on my newest acquisition?"

"No," I said, striding forward to stop right in front of him. Blinking, he took a step back. "Podium will be sold to Celeste Rhodes and TechWeb. You've lost the bid and the company." I couldn't resist a cold smile as his arrogant smirk faded into disbelief.

"*Quoi?*" he spat out, his nostrils flaring. "I cannot possibly have been outbid."

"Our decision has been made and is final." I put every ounce of steel I owned into the sentence.

Laurent drew himself up tall. "You are making a grave mistake. Your little company will soon be forgotten in the hands of that... Californian woman."

"It'll be a cold day in hell before we sell Podium to you," I said with ice-cold menace.

"And don't underestimate Celeste," Nate added. "We think she'll do wonders with the company. Some things are more important than money—Clay and I both have plenty of that." He joined my side, a nasty smile rising. "And best of all, you lost."

The Frenchman lifted his head to stare down his nose at us. "I have lost nothing."

"You can't resist being the center of attention, can you?" I asked. "You have to get your two cents in, even in situations that don't concern you. At all."

Understanding flashed over his face. Laurent sneered, his eyes narrowing as he glanced between us. "Ah... I see what is going on here. This is about your assistant, isn't it? You are a fool, Clay, letting your emotions dictate your decisions."

My jaw tightened, but I refused to let him bait me. "And what's the alternative? To be an aloof asshole with zero emotional depth like you? No, thanks. And thank God I figured that out in time. Your presence here is no longer needed."

As we turned to leave, Laurent shouted after us, his face red with rage. "As you wish! I'm calling my pilot and flying out of this... shithole immediately. I can assure you both you're making a terrible error. One you will deeply regret."

"Save your breath," Nate called back dismissively. "You were so busy thinking we couldn't turn down your offer that you never even considered that Clay and I could buy every company you own. Consider yourself lucky we've got better things to do."

We walked away, leaving Laurent fuming inside.

Strolling down the path flanked by manicured croton plants, I let a sense of triumph and relief wash over me.

Nate stretched both hands over his head, grinning as we walked. "Man, that felt awesome. Great way to start the day."

I let a humorless smile rise. "It was. And Podium is much better off now."

But there was still one more person I needed to convince, and Camille's words caromed off the inside of my head. "*Elise doesn't need to reassure you of her sincerity. You need to reassure her.*"

My steps slowed.

Nate followed my silent train of thought and gripped my shoulder. "I'll go talk to Celeste and tell her TechWeb is the new owner of Podium. You go straighten things out with Elise."

I halted. "You sure? I should really be there. I don't want Celeste to feel slighted that I didn't show."

Nate affected an insulted look as he smacked me on the shoulder hard enough to make me stagger. "Have you forgotten? I'm the charming one! She won't even realize you're not there."

Laughing, I conceded. "Go to it, then. And thanks."

He gave me a wave as he turned away. "Good luck."

I marched toward our cottage. *Our.* How easily that plural came to me. Since returning to Calypso Key, something had been stretched within me. And now it couldn't go back to its former shape. I smiled crookedly as I gave that something a name. As corny as it sounded, Elise had changed the shape of my heart.

And it was time to convince her of that.

Chapter Twenty-Two

Elise

I SAT on the plush couch, my laptop balanced on my knees as I tried to concentrate on last-minute details about the gala. The cottage living room was cozy and inviting around me, but I barely noticed my surroundings. I twirled my hair into a bun atop my head and adjusted my computer glasses. My fingers flew across the keyboard in a hopeless attempt at distraction.

The memory of Clay's shocked, hurt expression haunted me. When he'd told me to stay here while he met with Nate and they made their final decision, I knew it was because of what I'd said. Was I being a coward? Or maybe he was right, and I really was being unfair to him. Why did I have such a hard time believing we could make it work?

I snorted and set my laptop on the coffee table, closing it softly. "Because I live in the real world. And so does he. A very different world than mine." I hadn't yet cleaned up the remains of my angel. And if I needed any sign from the universe, there it was.

Yet my insides were twisting in tight little knots, tying and untying at the thought of what I'd done. What I'd stopped. Maybe we could straighten the whole mess out after the gala.

The cottage door shutting made me jump. I snapped my head up to Clay, returning to the room sooner than expected, and I made a squeaking sound in surprise. He stopped just inside, his handsome face wearing an expression of uncertainty and hesitation, so unlike his usual attitude. And that pause as he halted across the room caused heat to ignite in my body. Not the good kind of heat. This was worry, concern, and maybe even a little shame.

"Hi," I said softly. "What happened?"

He stared me in the eye as he walked over and sat on the couch next to me. "A big part of my life just got settled, and now I need to work on the other one. Nate and I just told Laurent he lost Podium."

My brows flew up. I was delighted at the news, and I hadn't been at all positive Clay would choose to look beyond the financial rewards. "Really? And how do you feel about that?"

"Good. Confident. Celeste is the right person for Podium and her offer is still pretty incredible. Nate and I worked our asses off to build that company, and Laurent wouldn't care about it." Sitting back, he scrubbed both hands through his hair, leaving it sticking up. Then he barked a laugh. "I just achieved what I've been working the last six months solid for. I sold Podium for a stunning price to someone who will do everything possible to ensure it continues to be a success. And you know what?" He slowly rolled his head to stare at me.

My mouth went dry. "What?"

"I don't give a shit about it. Any of it. I still don't understand what's happened to me since I came down here. But I've changed, and you're the reason why."

I hardly knew how to respond, and I laced my trembling fingers together. "You have changed. I'm not sure the Clay Harmon I knew in New York would have overlooked Laurent's higher offer."

"I realized that I was so furious at him because of how he treated you. He's been an ass since we arrived, and I don't mind when it's directed at me. But I won't put up with you being spoken to like that. I really gave him hell when I told him he lost."

My lips formed a smile, genuine warmth replacing my hollow regret. "I'm sure you did. And thanks for doing what you did. I think Celeste will do great things with the company."

"Podium hardly matters to me right now." He took a long breath and paused, searching my face. "Elise, *you're* what matters to me. I've felt more alive in the past few days and... happier than I have been in years. I've let work rule my life for so long, but here I remembered. What it felt like to enjoy the moment, the simple things. To relax. And I don't want to give it up. I don't want to give you up."

I stared at him, trying to absorb his words. And to believe I wasn't dreaming this. "Do you really mean that?"

"Yes. Every word," he said firmly. "We've started something here, and I don't want it to end. But you're right about one thing. It's not a good idea to date your immediate boss. So how about a new title for you? I'm going to purchase GreenDrive, and I could use a... transition specialist. I could set GreenDrive up as a separate company, so you could be independent and definitely not my assistant."

His words made my heart soar and set off alarm bells in equal measure. Our argument replayed in my head. "You accused me of using you to gain a promotion last night. You pretty much threw it in my face."

He took my hand. "Because I was being a prick, and I was hurt. I'm sorry. I know you better than that."

Finally, I let a smile form and squeezed his hand back. "I didn't mean to hurt you. I'm sorry too. I've spent my whole life struggling, trying to prove myself. I couldn't dare let myself... believe."

Sincerity was etched all over that handsome face. "Please believe. What do you think of my idea about GreenDrive?"

"Well, it sounds like a dream come true. But what's a transition specialist?"

"I have no idea," he admitted, his smile tinged with sheepishness. "I just made it up on the spot. But we can find something for you that's independent and outside my day-to-day activities. I want this to be your position, Elise. Because you've earned it through merit. Nothing else."

I cleared my throat over a sudden constriction. "Having you recognize that means a lot to me. Thank you."

"Don't thank me. I meant what I said. I hate to lose the best assistant I've ever had, but you deserve to shine. And I need you to understand something else. I don't give a damn what anyone thinks about us. People will talk and form opinions no matter what." He reached out and pulled the pin from my bun, spilling my hair and running his fingers through the tresses. "I promise I won't ever let anyone mistreat you. Not Bart. Not Laurent. No one."

"I know you won't. After all, you're my prince, aren't you?"

He winced, then laughed. "Not sure I acted too prince-like last night and this morning, but maybe I can make up for it." He twirled a lock of my hair around his finger. "I know you don't believe in fairy tales. But who says happily-ever-after can't happen in real life? My eyes have opened since we've arrived. Every fantastic, sexy, wonderful thing that's happened... has been when we've been together. You are gorgeous beyond words, but you're much more than that. You're smart, loyal, and you care about those around you. I'm a better man when I'm with you, and I like that."

A soft, fuzzy ball formed in my stomach at his words. Clay tightened his hold, his eyes becoming guarded, uncertain again. "Will you accept the new position? More importantly, will you accept... me?"

My heart swelled, and I nodded. "Yes. To both. Though we're really going to have to figure out what a transition specialist is."

"There will be plenty of time for that once we get back to New York." Relief flooded his chiseled features as he leaned toward me. Our lips met in a long, tender kiss that sent hope rushing through every cell in my body.

I pulled back with a smile and said, "But we still have a gala to pull off, you know."

Clay shook his head, his eyes becoming smoldering as he skated a finger down the side of my neck. A quake shuddered through me, and he brushed his thumb across my bottom lip. "Later. I don't care about the gala right now. All I care about is you. And I'm going to prove it to you."

He stood and pulled me to my feet, his hand warm outside mine as he led me into my bedroom. Not his. He was leading us to my room because he wanted me to feel secure. Confident.

Once inside, he gently removed my glasses and kissed me again, his hands cradling my face. Pulling away, he remained silent as his eyes traveled down my body and back up. He fanned my hair out and I closed my eyes, luxuriating in the gentle pulling sensation.

"Do you have any idea how sexy you are?" he asked. "God, you turn me on."

I stood still as he slowly undressed me, his fingertips sending a live current over my newly exposed skin everywhere he touched. A caress down my arm, a brush of fingers down my back, not only was it arousing, it was... caring. But as his lips met mine again, arousal won out. Each piece of clothing he removed increased the heat between us, our breaths growing heavier. I removed his shirt and kissed him back, rubbing my breasts against his chest, and couldn't resist a breathy moan.

He traced a finger across my shoulder, his touch featherlight and delicate. I closed my eyes, becoming lost in the sensation. Then I gasped when he pinched the tip of my breast. My eyes flew open, and he broke into a smile that sent liquid heat straight through me. The world outside the cottage disappeared, leaving only the two of us as we removed the rest of our clothing.

We slid into my bed, the soft sheets barely registering against my heated skin. I ruffled my hands through his thick hair as I pulled his head down, his lips silky against mine. He stroked my breast in a long, languid motion that only inflamed me more. This time I didn't want foreplay—I wanted connection. I wanted him inside me. Now.

"Clay," I whispered urgently, my voice thick with need.

He understood. Reaching into his wallet, he pulled out a condom and rolled it on.

He entered me slowly, his hand slowly stroking from my hip down my thigh. We were gentle at first. Our bodies moved together, once again reunited. He gently pressed his lips against my closed eyes, his warm breath tickling my skin.

"Oh, the things I'm going to do to you in my bed at home," he murmured as he pushed hard, increasing his rhythm.

"I can't wait," I replied, his words—and his motions—stoking the fire deep within me.

He looked into my eyes, still moving within me. "Do you believe now?"

My heart raced as I stared back, the pull between us inescapable. Our bodies moved together with perfect synchronization, nothing like two new lovers. The intensity of his gaze felt electric as we fused together in a moment of raw, deep emotion.

"Yes, I believe. You're my prince."

He laughed against my ear, the warm puff of air making my toes curl. "Only yours."

Our passion built further, and I rolled on top of him, straddling his hips as I took control. I spread my fingers across his pecs, brushing the soft hair as I moved above him. With a deep moan, he folded forward, placing his fingers between my legs as he left a line of wet kisses across my collarbone. The contact made me cry out, the sound echoing in the dim room. He doubled his efforts.

"That's it," he whispered in my ear. "More. I want to hear you."

I moved faster, and he gripped me behind my back, urging me to press hard against his hand. My orgasm built like a tidal wave, each stroke of his fingers pushing me higher. Each surge within me urging me closer. I ground myself against him, desperate for more. And he gave it to me, panting my name in my ear as we went over the edge together. We froze, arms tightening around each other. A sense of completion washed over me as I cried out into the silent room.

Belief.

Confidence.

We slowly wound down, our sweat-slicked bodies pressed together. Then we settled back under the covers with me half on top. I stroked his chest, feeling the contrast between the strength beneath his skin and the tenderness he'd shown me. I stretched out on top of him, snuggling close as he wrapped both arms around me and held me tight.

Chapter Twenty-Three

Clay

A CONTENTED SIGH escaped me as I shifted slightly, pulling Elise closer. The sheets were wrapped around us, our bodies still warm and damp. A sense of peace, of deep fulfillment, settled over me, unlike anything I'd ever experienced. I'd always prided myself on my control, my ability to compartmentalize, but being with Elise... she made me forget about everything but the two of us.

I opened my eyes, my gaze drawn to the bright sunlight streaming through the sliding glass door. It sparkled off the surface of the pool, beckoning us back into its cool embrace. But to hell with that—I was too comfortable.

"I hope you realize how much I appreciate you," I breathed against her neck. "At work, you've always been there when I needed you. And now you're so much more."

"I think *we're* so much more. With more to come."

As I slowly brushed my hand over the soft curve of her hip, my eye snagged on something white on the floor near the dresser. It looked like a pile of broken pieces as I pushed myself up on one elbow. "What's that?"

Elise followed my gaze, a shadow crossing her face. "My angel," she murmured. "It fell off the dresser and..." She trailed off, then shrugged with a sad smile.

"It broke?"

"Into pieces. It happened right after our argument and I was so upset, I didn't even bother to pick them up. It seemed like a sign, you know?"

"What do you mean?" I asked, drawing my brows together.

Her gaze drifted toward the shattered fragments. "I took it as a sign that I wasn't listening to my history." She paused. "My instinct has always been to depend on myself, to build my own security, to not rely on anyone else. And that little angel... I told you the story. It was symbolic to me."

"That you should trust no one?"

"Not exactly," she said, a wry smile curving her lips. "More like... trust myself. Create my own destiny. Fairy tales are for children, Clay. And I grew up early." She shook her head, a strand of hair falling across her cheek. I reached out, my fingers brushing the soft strands away.

"But here we are," she whispered, her dark blue eyes meeting mine, a spark of something—Hope? Wonder?— lighting them from within.

"Maybe it *was* a sign," I said, the thought coming to me. "A sign that you're ready to let go of those old beliefs. To take a leap of faith. To embrace something... new."

Her smile widened, and she snuggled closer, resting her head on my chest. "I like that idea," she murmured. "I like it a lot."

She kept repeating that statement about life not being a fairy tale. I was hardly a sentimental man, but damn if she didn't make me want to ensure every dream she'd ever had came true. And an idea formed in my head...

Elise breathed out a long, drawn-out sigh before cracking an eye to look at the digital clock on the nightstand. "I could stay like this forever. But I guess we'd better get back to the gala, huh?"

"Probably a good idea," I agreed with a gentle laugh, brushing a stray hair from her forehead. "The clock is ticking down, Cinderella."

THE BALLROOM BUZZED with activity as I strolled through the open French doors two hours later, taking in the scene with a sense of detached amusement. Resort staff members hurried about, their movements a blur of purposeful chaos. Tables were being draped in crisp white linen, chairs arranged around them, and glittering gold and black streamers hung from the soaring ceiling. The air was thick with the scent of lilies and orchids, a heady fragrance that usually would have given me a headache. But today, it seemed to blend with the gentle hum of excitement, creating an atmosphere of anticipation, of possibility.

I was dressed casually—the formalwear would come later. A pale blue Ralph Lauren polo shirt hugged my shoulders, and my khaki cargo shorts were loose and comfortable. After a long, leisurely shower—with Elise, of course—I'd opted for practicality. There was still a lot to oversee before tonight's event, and comfort was key. I ran a hand over my hair, the strands still damp, and caught the lingering scent of Elise's coconut shampoo.

I spotted Nate and Camille across the room near a long table, meticulously arranging a collection of candles and hurricane vases, their laughter echoing through the ballroom. As Nate climbed a ladder to adjust some crepe paper, Camille looked up and smiled.

"Clay!" she said, her smile widening as I approached. "You're looking awfully relaxed for a man about to put the final touches on the sale of his company."

I laughed, the sound deeper and more carefree than usual. "Just enjoying the tropical air, I guess." My gaze was drawn to Elise. She was conferring with a group of staff members near the stage, her back to me. Even from this distance, I could sense her focused energy.

My gaze lingered. She was dressed in fitted black capris and a sleeveless white blouse, her auburn hair pulled back in a practical clip, her glasses on her nose. She was all business, her movements precise and efficient as she adjusted a spotlight, her voice clear and authoritative as she gave instructions to the staff.

And yet... she looked so incredibly sexy. How had I never noticed that before? I'd always appreciated Elise's competence, her unwavering dedication to her work. But seeing her now, in her element, her intelligence and passion shining through, I was struck by a new awareness. She was a woman who commanded my attention, my respect, and... something deeper.

"Enjoyment must be contagious," Camille observed, her voice laced with knowing amusement. "I've noticed Elise has been very chipper this afternoon. Looks like someone might have listened to me."

"I did," I said, my gaze still fixed on Elise. Then I turned and bowed. "Thank you, Camille. Your advice was spot on."

Surprise flickered across her face, a rare crack in her usual composure. Before she could respond, Nate stepped down from the ladder, a mischievous grin on his face.

"Camille, baby, you'd never believe this, but Clay actually has a heart beating beneath that titanium exterior. And he's always been willing to give credit where it's due." He came over and clapped me on the shoulder. "Love does a body good, doesn't it, brother?"

"We've only been together a few days," I said, my tone deliberately light as I shrugged off his comment.

"Okay, okay," Nate said, holding his hands up in mock surrender. "Point taken. But I've never seen you this… mellow. You're usually pacing the floor and barking orders at everyone before a big event." He paused, tilting his head toward Elise with a sly grin. "It's kind of cute, actually. Though I still can't believe you're wearing *shorts*. At a work event! What would our investors say?"

I frowned at my legs, then raised my eyes to his. "They won't see me, now, will they? I assure you, I'll be impeccably dressed tonight."

"I'd never guess you would be the type who enjoys event prep," Camille observed.

"You're telling me," Nate chimed in, shaking his head. "This is a man who schedules his bathroom breaks."

"Would you two shut up?" My tone came out exasperated, but when they started laughing, I joined in. "Okay, fair point. About the event planning, not the bathroom schedule! Usually, I'd rather be anywhere else. But…" I paused, my gaze drawn back to Elise, who was now adjusting the microphone on the stage. "This is a special occasion."

As our eyes met, a smile touched her lips, and I couldn't help but grin back. Very unbusiness-like thoughts began running through my head, and I blinked, making a determined effort to concentrate on the gala.

I turned as Camille clapped her hands together. "This is

so great," she said, her voice filled with genuine happiness. "I'm so happy for you both."

Nate, his usual playful grin replaced by a sincere smile, stepped forward and shook my hand. "Me too, brother. You deserve a little happiness."

My mind drifted to what I had planned for tonight. All of it. "Tonight is going to be very special," I said, unable to keep the excitement from creeping into my voice.

"Oh, I'm sure it will be," Nate said with a big smile full of mischief.

A few minutes later, Elise approached us, clipboard in hand. Her cheeks were flushed but her eyes sparkled, even in the midst of controlled chaos.

"Everything's on track," she said, her gaze sweeping over the ballroom. "The catering staff is setting up the buffet, the band is doing their sound check, and the guest list has been confirmed. I talked to the Podium staff who flew in for the party, and everyone is here and getting ready. Just a few last-minute details to finalize."

"Excellent work as usual," I said, my gaze meeting hers. I couldn't help but reach out, my fingers brushing lightly against her arm as I took the clipboard from her. It was a subtle touch, barely noticeable in the bustling activity of the ballroom, but she tipped me a wink in response.

"Look at you two," Camille teased, her gaze darting between Elise and me. "Who knew fairy tales could happen in real life?"

Elise laughed, shaking her head, but her cheeks reddened. "Maybe happy endings. Fairy tales are still a stretch."

"Give it time, honey," Camille said, a twinkle glinting in her eye. "One of these days, you'll be trading in that practical clipboard for a magic wand."

Elise laughed and shook her head. "Honestly, Camille, I can't imagine anything more magical than what's happened over the past few days."

A giddy, ridiculous happiness spread through me at her words, and I found myself wanting to pull her close, to kiss her right there in the middle of the bustling ballroom. But I held back, my gaze catching Nate's knowing grin. There would be time for that later. Tonight was about more than stolen kisses and whispered promises. Tonight was about... everything.

"Mr. Harmon?" Evan Markham appeared nearby wearing a hesitant smile as he stared at me.

Nate burst into laughter. "It's funny. There are two Mr. Harmons here, yet I never have any question about where I stand."

Alarm filled Evan's eyes, but I just waved him off. "Ignore Nate. He's just trying to play on your sympathy. Don't take the bait."

Nate shrugged unapologetically and grinned at Evan. "Speaking of sympathy, or lack of—what happened with our dear Laurent DuBois?"

The general manager's face took on a pained expression before he quickly covered it. "He and his companion just left the resort a short while ago. Housekeeping is, uh, cleaning up his room."

I allowed a grim, satisfied smile to rise on my face at the vision of the insufferable jerk wrecking his surroundings in a fit of rage. "I assure you I'm happy to pay for any damage he caused. Perhaps we should discuss it in private?"

"Of course. I'm at your convenience." Evan held my gaze, his manner giving no indication that he'd picked up the signal I was sending. The man was a pro—I had to give him that.

I glanced at my watch and nodded as I swept my gaze over our little group. "Whatever damage Laurent did, the end result was worth the cost." My eyes halted on Elise's and my heart gave a little jump. "See you in a few hours."

Then I followed Evan out of the ballroom, the busy, festive atmosphere fading behind me as I stepped into the quiet hallway. As soon as we had privacy, he and I got to work. Tonight, more than just Podium's future was at stake.

Tonight, I was betting on a different kind of magic.

Chapter Twenty-Four

Elise

AS I STEPPED across the floor of the private ballroom at Orchid, the atmosphere enveloped me like a warm embrace—the results of our afternoon. Shimmering gold and black streamers adorned the walls, meeting in the ceiling and announcing New Year's Eve in all its grandeur. The white marble floor shone beneath my feet, reflecting the twinkle of the chandeliers above. Black-and-gold helium-filled balloons danced across the ceiling, blown by a gentle breeze wafting through the open windows. Tropical hardwood ceiling beams arched elegantly overhead and framed the lush potted orchids that graced the walls. In one corner, a band played soft calypso music while couples swayed on the dance floor.

As I walked through the room, my gaze fell upon Clay, looking as if he'd just stepped off the cover of a magazine in his tailored Brioni tuxedo. Hair perfectly groomed and the definition of tall, dark, and handsome, he was the walking embodiment of raw power and success. That small voice inside me tried to speak up, but I quashed it. Clay had proven himself to me. What more convincing could I possibly need?

I'd continued with the ball preparations after he and Evan stepped out. Then I got dressed and arrived at Orchid early, just to make sure nothing was amiss. As I panned my gaze around the room, I had to admit it was all perfect. I didn't know what the future held, but I couldn't believe the changes just a few days had brought. The new position I'd been working toward. And best of all, Clay.

The man, not the mogul.

My heart nearly stopped when he caught sight of me, his eyes sliding up and down my body. Closing the distance between us, he subtly touched the small of my back, sending a thrill down my spine.

"You look absolutely stunning tonight," he whispered near my ear, his rich voice full of warmth before he pulled back to a respectable distance.

His words made me flush, and I smiled at the compliment. I was dressed for the occasion with my hair styled in an elaborate updo and a sparkling silver evening gown hugging my curves. My matching high heels clicked against the floor, and I almost felt like a fairy-tale princess myself.

I let my eyes linger on him. "Thank you. As much as I've enjoyed getting to know Casual Clay the last few days, you're impeccable in a tux."

He bowed crisply, somehow managing to look dashing and not like a butler. My attention shifted to an elaborate wall clock that hung nearby, its hands indicating it was now closing in on midnight. Nate and Camille snuck out a side door facing the beach, practically tiptoeing. Clay and I exchanged glances, wondering where they were off to.

With a shrug, Clay said, "It's their loss if they want to miss the big event. It's time to get the show on the road."

He tipped me a wink, and affection for him surged through me. We had been circumspect tonight, reverting to our traditional roles during the gala. I didn't want to detract from his well-deserved celebration, but I couldn't deny how much I appreciated the subtle glances and fleeting touches he'd given me throughout the evening.

"Are you ready?" I asked him quietly. "You've been waiting a long time for this."

"More than ever."

With that, Clay took a glass of champagne from a passing server and stepped onto the stage in front of the microphone. The room quieted as everyone faced him, anticipation hanging in the air. A resort employee set a soft-pink box on a stool next to him, its contents hidden from view, which piqued my interest. This wasn't on our checklist.

"Good evening, everyone," Clay began, his voice steady and confident. "I'd like to raise my glass to Celeste Rhodes."

Wearing a lovely dark-blue dress, she beamed up at him. Her husband stood on one side of her and her white-haired father on the other, both in tuxedos.

"Congratulations, Celeste! I am confident Podium is in excellent hands and its future will be limitless. And we're delighted your father and husband could make the trip and celebrate with us as well."

As he spoke, I smiled at how he refrained from mentioning anything financial. The sales price had been fifteen billion dollars—a figure that would become public knowledge soon enough. Laurent's offer had been twenty billion.

"Cheers to all of you as well," he continued, toasting the

audience. The room erupted in resounding applause, glasses clinking together in celebration. Clay had flown all of Podium's senior staff in his private jet to attend the gala, not wanting anyone to miss what they had worked so hard to accomplish.

"Podium has always been a family business," he told Celeste, his voice filled with sincerity. "I hope it will continue to be that way under your leadership."

Celeste smiled warmly and called out, "We've been planning to open a New York office, and now we have the perfect excuse! Rest assured, all Podium employees will remain on board."

The audience cheered even louder. My heart swelled for the man on stage. He had dedicated so much of himself to Podium, and this night was a testament to his success.

"None of this would have been possible without the incredibly hard work and dedication of everyone in this room," Clay continued, then smiled. "I'd like to thank my brother, who has disappeared at the most important moment, which is pretty typical." He paused as laughter rippled through the room. "But without Nate's presence and hard work, Podium would never have become what it is today."

Then his eyes settled on me. "Finally, I want to acknowledge Elise Briggs, whose contribution was invaluable." Our eyes locked, and my heart skipped a beat. A blush crept up my cheeks as more applause sounded.

"Elise, you've been by my side for three years, and you've worked nonstop on Podium for the past year. None of this would be happening without you."

He paused, inhaling deeply as he let his gaze linger on the view outside the open doors. "Returning to Calypso Key represents a very real turning point in my life. I arrived a very different man than I'll be leaving. And that's a good thing. In a very short time, Elise, you've shown me there's more to life than work. I've let that slip away, but now that I've got a firm grasp on it again... I'm not about to let life—or you—get away."

The room erupted in applause once more, a low murmur rippling through it, and tears filled my eyes. People shifted away from me, leaving me the center of attention. My hesitations about his sincerity were in the past now, but seeing him on stage like this was beyond my wildest imagination.

After a final smile at me, Clay addressed the audience again. "Elise is fond of saying that life isn't a fairy tale, and she didn't believe our story could have a happy ending. She even referred to me as a prince, if you can believe that." He shrugged, a playful grin crossing his face. "So I figured, if I'm supposed to be Prince Charming, I might as well act the part."

He turned to the soft-pink box beside him. It was about a foot square with an elaborate white bow on top. He lifted the lid. The audience collectively gasped as he pulled out a glass slipper, glittering and shimmering under the spotlights.

"So, I have a bargain for you, Elise," he said, pinning me with his eyes. "If the slipper fits, will you finally believe in happy endings?"

A spotlight was trained on me, and I realized my mouth was hanging open. Snapping it shut, I forced my feet to move. In a daze, I climbed onto the stage. My legs were shaky, but I managed to reach Clay, whose eyes never left mine. Growing quiet, the audience crowded closer, eager to watch the show unfold.

With a trembling leg, I shook off my right shoe. The

cold marble of the stage bit into my bare foot, grounding me in reality even as my mind swirled with disbelief. Clay hunkered down before me, holding the glass slipper. I laughed as that lock of hair sprang free across his forehead and he casually swept it back into place. As he placed my foot inside, the slipper seemed to mold itself around me like a glove.

A perfect fit.

The crowd roared, their excitement echoing through the ballroom. I burst into laughter, holding my hands against my mouth as Clay reached into the box and removed a second slipper. He carefully placed it on my other foot before rising again, his smile contagious. I could hardly believe what had just happened, and yet, here I was, standing on a stage in front of a crowd of people with two glass slippers on my feet.

"When? How... did you make this happen?" My quiet words were halting, dumbfounded.

Instead of replying, Clay merely winked at me. After a glance at the wall clock, he took my hand and led me back to the microphone. I moved in a daze, every detail in the room both impossibly vivid and ephemeral.

"It's a couple of minutes to midnight," he announced, "so let's all hit the dance floor and welcome the New Year in style!"

As the band broke into a soft, tropical tune, we made our way to the center of the dance floor. I could have been floating on air except for the solid clicks my perfectly fitting heels made against the floor. Couples surrounded us, dancing to the music, but all I could focus on was the man before me. The man who'd just turned my life into a fairy tale.

The world around us slowed, fading to background

noise as Clay and I swayed together on the dance floor. I'd never seen him dance, but I wasn't surprised that he moved gracefully and easily. My school dance lessons came back to me, and the perfect vision was maintained as I glided in his arms. His gaze never left mine, and his hand gently traced the small of my back. Goose bumps pebbled both of my arms. The soft music enveloped us, creating an intimate cocoon that made me forget the people celebrating all around us.

"Ten... nine... eight..."

The crowd began counting down in the background, their voices a distant murmur to my ears. Our lips drew closer, drawn together like magnets.

"Seven... six... five... four..."

"Yes," I whispered, my heart pounding in my chest. I couldn't believe this was happening, that this man who had only seen me as his assistant for so long was now inches away from kissing me very publicly.

"Three... two... one..."

The anticipation built, electrifying the air between us.

"Happy New Year!"

Everyone shouted, and at that moment, our lips met. My arms found their way around Clay's neck, while his wrapped around my waist, pulling me even closer to him.

Our kiss deepened, fueled by the emotions we were both experiencing. His body was warm against mine, and his embrace was firm and confident. Time stood still as we lost ourselves in each other, standing on the dance floor and encased in our own enchanted world.

Eventually, the cheering crowd broke through, and I realized they weren't just celebrating the arrival of the new year—they were cheering for us. Sheepishly, I pulled away from Clay and offered a smile to our friends and colleagues.

"Thank you," I murmured, heat warming my face.

"Let's keep dancing," Clay suggested, his eyes full of mirth as he led me back into the rhythm of the music. "So did I pull it off?"

I started to speak, but only a squeak came out. I cleared my throat and tried again, still in awe of the evening's events. "How did you do all this?"

His grin took up half of his face. "Evan wasn't kidding when he said he could make anything happen. And I'm not exactly a slouch in that department either, you know. I'm not sure exactly how he got the slippers made so fast, but he did. After we left the meeting this afternoon, I snuck out one of your shoes to use as a size guide and Evan did the rest."

I laughed, still in shock. "This is the most amazing thing that's ever happened to me."

"Then I've done my job," he said, pulling me closer. We danced to the obligatory "Auld Lang Syne", staring into each other's eyes as the first moments of the new year unfolded around us. Clay leaned down to capture my lips once more, and I threw my arms around his neck. Still kissing, he picked me up and spun me around him in a circle. Both of us started laughing.

Our mirth was interrupted as Nate and Camille appeared next to us, looking somewhat flushed but with wide grins on their faces. "Looks like we missed something big," Nate said with a grin.

Clay frowned at him. "Yeah. The entire speech, countdown, and celebration. Where have you two been?"

Camille's lovely smile widened as she held up her left hand, displaying a sparkling diamond ring on her finger. "Having our own celebration. We're engaged!"

"Congratulations!" I screeched, momentarily forgetting

my own surprise and delight as I threw my arms around Camille. She hugged me back, her eyes shining.

"Congrats, little brother," Clay said, shaking Nate's hand. "Looks like the Harmon boys managed to do pretty well in the end, doesn't it?"

As I slid against him, I looked up into his eyes, still a pale blue but not so icy anymore. "I can't imagine any happier ending."

We shared another kiss, this one sweet and tender, and moved to the rhythm once more. Nate and Camille danced alongside us. The soft music played around us, and the intoxicating scent of orchids filled the air. As I stared out the open window at the gentle ocean, a meteor bolted across the sky in a long, white streak.

I didn't need to make a wish.

Epilogue

Clay

ONE YEAR LATER

THE PRIVATE BEACH was on a small, deserted key. The scene was picture-perfect, with swaying palm trees overhead and powdery soft white sand. As the sun began to cast a deep orange glow across the sky, I eased out a contented sigh, taking in the beauty and tranquility surrounding Elise and me. We sat on a blanket as we watched the sunset unfold. An employee from Calypso Key Resort had dropped us off earlier, giving us the opportunity to enjoy this serene, but very private, escape, and would return for us an hour from now.

Elise leaned into my side, her head resting on my shoulder. We sat in contented silence, savoring the last of the champagne in our glasses. So much had changed in the year since we first came to Calypso Key. Yet returning to where we started, it felt as though nothing had changed at all.

The remains of our dinner spread out before us on the blanket. I gazed down at Elise, my breath stuck in my lungs. Her hair fell around her shoulders in soft waves, her eyes reflecting the vibrant colors of the sunset.

She caught me staring and smiled. "What?"

"Just thinking about how lucky I am." Anticipation coursed through me, making my heart race. "For you and what we have together."

Her smile widened. "The feeling's mutual."

Three months ago, we moved into a brand-new three-bedroom condo. My old place was stark and harsh, and her flat in Queens could barely fit two people. And though I didn't grow up rich, I fully enjoyed the privileges my money provided. So we bought a new penthouse unit. This one also huge and overlooking Central Park, but we chose the finishes together and the space reflected the harmonious blending of our lives. Gone were my cold, severe, modern designs, replaced by Elise's straight lines softened with cozy touches that made our space feel like a true home.

I smiled, reaching over to tuck a stray lock of hair behind her ear. "I'm glad I was able to surprise you with this trip. You've been working too hard lately, and I'd like to remind you there's more to life than work."

Elise laughed softly, leaning into my touch. "You're right, but I still have to laugh at you saying those words. Though I didn't mind helping Nate and Camille with Skate to Success. I love organizing and the absolute rocket launch of their foundation took everyone by surprise. It didn't add much to my workload."

My brother's venture after hockey had proved a smashing success, fully launching him into a thriving new career. Camille handled most of the day-to-day operations, leaving him free to spend his day on the ice, where he wanted to be. I had been Nate's best man and Elise Camille's maid of honor at their wedding in Westport five months ago.

"And I'm eternally grateful that neither of us worked Christmas," she said with a pointed look.

Laughing, I rubbed the back of my neck. "Yeah, I guess that was kind of a dick thing to do on my part, wasn't it?" I leaned over and kissed her brow. "No more working Christmases. I promise."

Elise raised her champagne flute to me. "Your timing was perfect for this little getaway. My engine will be fully recharged when we get back to New York, and I can focus on GreenDrive again."

My chest filled at how Elise had worked her way into a prominent position at GreenDrive, purely on the merit of her own hard work and skill. I'd taken a completely hands-off approach to my new company, installing an independent CEO and telling him to consider Elise like any other employee. After making sure he knew she was the center of my life, of course.

A tiger can't change his stripes, after all.

But I could have kept my mouth shut, and it wouldn't have changed anything. I studied the quarterly reports carefully. Elise had prospered and worked her way up the ladder in less than a year. For my part, I'd begun a new start-up over the past year, an app that helped people find lower-cost, clean energy alternatives. It was already more successful than Podium had been in its early days.

I drew Elise closer, breathing in the faint scent of coconut from the sunscreen she'd applied earlier. We'd spent two days scuba diving with April, exploring the crystalline waters that had brought us together. Private dinners in our cottage and romantic candlelit meals at Orchid reminded us of our first trip. We made love in our cottage as the waves lapped at the shore, a soothing rhythm that lulled us to sleep each night, wrapped in each other's arms.

Tightening my arms around her, I rested my cheek against her hair. "I love you. More every day."

"I love you too," she replied. Her smile stretched the soft skin of her cheek. "Thank you for always knowing exactly what I need, even before I do."

"That's what I'm here for," I said. "It's not easy being a prince. You keep me on my toes."

Elise squeezed my hand, her laugh filling the twilight. "You'll always be my prince."

As the sun kissed the horizon, a warm palette of oranges, pinks, and purples painted the sky. The sea's gentle waves lapped upon the sand, each one leaving a glistening trail that reflected the colors above. A fluttery thrill built within me.

I touched her arm. "Let's go for a sunset stroll along the beach."

"I'd love to."

We slipped off our shoes and stepped onto the soft, warm sand. As we walked hand in hand, the water washed over our bare feet, the warmth surprising. The ocean was warmer than the air by this time of the evening. Fine grains of sand slipped between my toes, grounding me in the moment. I cast my gaze over the scattering of shells on the shoreline, smiling to myself when I spotted a large conch shell half-buried in the sand.

"Look at that," I said, nodding toward the intriguing find. Elise followed my gaze, her eyes lighting up as she saw the shell too.

"It's so beautiful," she exclaimed, dropping my hand to crouch down and pick it up. The shell was a stunning specimen, with a glowing pink interior that seemed to absorb the hues of the setting sun. She brushed her fingers over the smooth pink surface.

"Look at how perfect it is," she murmured, tipping the shell slightly. Then she frowned as a clinking sound emanated from within. She gasped. "There's not a crab in here, I hope!"

I grinned. "I think the opening is too small. What is it?"

She tilted the shell further, cupping her hand under the open end. A three-carat princess-cut diamond ring tumbled out, landing gracefully in her palm.

Elise stared down at the ring, her mouth agape. She lifted her eyes to meet mine.

I plucked the ring from her hand and lowered to one knee, feeling the sand settle beneath me as my heart threatened to pound out of my chest.

"We began here," I said, looking up into her wide eyes. "This is where you helped me discover that there's so much more to life than just work. Where I learned what it was to really live. For the last year, you have been my rock, my inspiration, and the love of my life. I can't imagine a future without you by my side."

Her eyes filled with tears, but she didn't interrupt. The only sound in the world was the waves lapping against the shore.

"Will you be my wife?"

A tear slid down her cheek, glistening in the fading light. She seemed at a loss for words, but her expression was eloquent enough. Finally, she nodded and shouted, "Yes, Clay. Yes, yes!"

I smiled, relief and a stunning lightness flooding

through me. I slipped the ring onto her finger, where it glimmered in the setting sun. A perfect fit, of course. As I stood up, Elise threw her arms around my neck, pulling me close for a long kiss.

"Such a perfect proposal," she murmured against my lips. Then she pulled back and gave me that smile I could never get tired of. "I love your surprises."

"Good," I replied, my heart too big for my chest. "Because I plan to keep surprising you for a very long time."

As the sun dipped below the horizon, we stood there, arms wrapped around each other. Our trip to Calypso Key had forever changed our lives, and now we would begin a new chapter together.

For now, though, I simply wanted to savor this moment. The sky continued to darken, stars peeking out one by one, while the gentle ocean serenaded us. The sounds of the water and rustling palm leaves created a soothing symphony of nature.

"Here's to fairy tales and happy endings," I murmured as I pulled her close. After whisking another soft kiss over her lips, we stood together under the watchful, velvety canopy of stars.

THANK you for reading CLOCK STRIKES PARADISE! I've been wanting to write a traditional billionaire romance for a while, and setting it at Calypso Key was the umbrella on the tropical drink! And the Cinderella retelling added such a fun element to the story.

If you're familiar with Calypso Key, I hope you enjoyed seeing old friends in the past two books. And if you're new to this beautiful little island in the Florida Keys, then I invite to to pick up a copy of VISIONS OF YOU!

This novel is a grumpy-sunshine, single dad romance between eldest son Gabe Markham and April Desmond, the newly hired divemaster he may need to fire:

VISIONS OF YOU: A Small Town Single Dad Romance
CALYPSO KEY SERIES

**I'm a single dad, not the prodigal son.
And that gorgeous, sunny blonde? She's just an
employee.**

GABE:

When Dad needs help running our family resort at Calypso Key, I can't say no. So I bring my daughter home to raise where I grew up. Except the resort is worse off than I expected. Still, I understand business. Women... not so much. And after my divorce, I don't believe in love.

Then I meet new divemaster April Desmond.

She was hired before I came back. I have one job—to cut costs everywhere I can. I try to deny the attraction. After all, I might have to fire her. But that sheet of golden hair. Those sky-blue eyes.

The sparks become an inferno. We're opposites in many ways. April is the sunshine to my grumpiness. But we agree on one thing—neither of us wants a serious relationship. We make a promise to keep things casual, and it works great.

Until one of us breaks our pact...

VISIONS OF YOU is available in ebook and enrolled in Kindle Unlimited, so you can read for free with your subscription. You can also get it in print and audio. Click below to grab your copy:

VISIONS OF YOU: A Small Town Single Dad Romance
CALYPSO KEY SERIES

IF YOU'D LIKE a glimpse into **Clay and Elise's future (as well as Nate and Camille's!)**, make sure you click below to sign up for my newsletter:

Beach Read Update
(www.erinbrockus.com/clock)

As a thank you, I'll send you a **bonus scene** which peeks into their happy future.

If you're already on my list, I've got you covered! At the bottom of each newsletter is a link to all my free content for subscribers. Just find your last email from me to read this bonus, as well as any others you might have missed. Or you can simply sign up again—you'll have your bonus in a flash.

ISLAND ESCAPES SERIES:

In Too Deep: A Second Chance Romance

Beached in Bali: A Friends to Lovers Romance

Betting on Paradise: A Fake Relationship Billionaire Romance

Clock Strikes Paradise: A Billionaire Cinderella-Retelling Romance

CALYPSO KEY SERIES:

Main Novels:

Visions of You: A Small Town Single Dad Romance

Because of You: A Small Town Fake Relationship Romance

Memories of You: A Small Town Second Chance Romance

Shades of You: A Small Town Forbidden Romance

ASSOCIATED SHORT STORIES AND NOVELLAS:

Traces of You: A Small Town Rivals to Lovers Romance*

* Subscriber exclusive

HALF MOON BAY SERIES:

MAIN NOVELS:

Finding Hope: Half Moon Bay Book 1

Defending Hope: Half Moon Bay Book 2

Rising Hope: Half Moon Bay Book 3

Forever Hope: Half Moon Bay Book 4

Half Moon Whim: Half Moon Bay Book 5 (Standalone)

Half Moon Ember: Half Moon Bay Book 6 (Standalone)

Half Moon Aqua: Half Moon Bay Book 7

Crowning Hope: Half Moon Bay Book 8

The Half Moon Bay Collection Books 1-4: The Hope and Alex Story

Associated Short Stories and Novellas:

Tropical Dawn: A Half Moon Bay Prequel Novella

*Tropical Chance**: A Second Chance Half Moon Bay Novella

*Tropical Hope**: A Half Moon Bay Prequel Short Story

* Subscriber exclusives

Dive into steamy small-town romance, where passion meets paradise!

Award-winning author Erin Brockus writes steamy small town romances that transport readers to exotic, tropical destinations, and provide a perfect beachy getaway from everyday life. Her mature, relatable characters are impossible not to root for, and she weaves breezy romantic adventure into her stories, emphasizing scuba diving and the ocean.

Drawing on her twin passions for diving and travel, Erin infuses her characters and narratives with a sense of excitement and passion. Her idea of the perfect day involves sipping a cocktail on the beach after exploring the ocean depths.

Erin lives in Washington wine country with her husband, who is also a scuba instructor. She is currently hard at work on her next island adventure. When she's not writing, she enjoys running, mountain biking, or enjoying a good book with a cup of coffee.